COLETTE

My Reading

MICHÈLE ROBERTS

COLETTE

My Literary Mother

OXFORD
UNIVERSITY PRESS

OXFORD
UNIVERSITY PRESS

Great Clarendon Street, Oxford, OX2 6DP,
United Kingdom

Oxford University Press is a department of the University of Oxford.
It furthers the University's objective of excellence in research, scholarship,
and education by publishing worldwide. Oxford is a registered trade mark of
Oxford University Press in the UK and in certain other countries

Published in the United States of America by Oxford University Press
198 Madison Avenue, New York, NY 10016, United States of America

British Library Cataloguing in Publication Data
Data available

Library of Congress Control Number: 2023950791

ISBN 9780192858214

DOI: 10.1093/oso/9780192858214.001.0001

Printed and bound by
CPI Group (UK) Ltd, Croydon, CR0 4YY

SERIES INTRODUCTION

This series is built on a simple presupposition: that it helps to have a book recommended and discussed by someone who cares for it. Books are not purely self-sufficient: they need people and they need to get to what is personal within them.

The people we have been seeking as contributors to *My Reading* are readers who are also writers: novelists and poets; literary critics, outside as well as inside universities, but also thinkers from other disciplines—philosophy, psychology, science, theology, and sociology—beside the literary; and, not least of all, intense readers whose first profession is not writing itself but, for example, medicine, or law, or a non-verbal form of art. Of all of them we have asked: what books or authors feel as though they are deeply *yours*, influencing or challenging your life and work, most deserving of rescue and attention, or demanding of feeling and use?

What is it like to love this book? What is it like to have a thought or idea or doubt or memory, not cold and in abstract, but live in the very act of reading? What is it like to feel, long after, that this writer is a vital part of your life? We ask our authors to respond to such bold questions by writing not conventionally but personally—whatever 'personal' might mean, whatever form or style it might take, for them as individuals. This does not mean overt confession at the expense of a chosen book or author; but nor should our writers be afraid of making autobiographical connections. What was wanted was whatever made for their own hardest thinking in careful relation to quoted sources and specifics. The work was to go on in the taut and resonant space between these readers and their chosen books. And the interest within that area begins precisely when it is no longer clear how much is coming from the text and how much is coming from its readers—where that distinction is no longer easily tenable because neither is sacrificed to the other. That would show what reading meant at its most serious and how it might have relation to an individual life.

Out of what we hope will be an ongoing variety of books and readers, *My Reading* offers personal models of what it is like to care about particular authors, to re-create through specific examples imaginative versions of what those authors and works represent, and to show their effect upon a reader's own thinking and development.

ANNE CHENG
PHILIP DAVIS
JACQUELINE NORTON
MARINA WARNER
MICHAEL WOOD

in memory of Monique Caulle Roberts

CONTENTS

ABBREVIATIONS

BD	Colette, *Break of Day*, trans. Enid McLeod (London: The Women's Press, 1979)
Ch.	Colette, *Chéri* (Paris: Livre de Poche, Fayard, 2021)
CFC	*Chéri* and *La Fin de Chéri*, trans. Roger Senhouse (Harmondsworth: Penguin Modern Classics, 1962)
CFF	Michèle Sarde, *Colette: Free and Fettered* (New York: William Morrow & Co., 1980)
FBB	Marina Warner, *From the Beast to the Blonde: On Fairy Tales and their Tellers* (London: Chatto and Windus, 1994)
FG	Claude Francis and Fernande Gontier, *Colette* (Paris: Librairie Académique Perrin, 1997)
LLP	*La Lune de pluie*, in Chambre d'hôtel suivi de La Lune de pluie (Paris: Livre de Poche, Fayard, 1954)
LMC	Colette, *La Maison de Claudine* (Paris: Livre de Poche/Librairie Hachette, 1960)
LNJ	Colette, *La Naissance du jour* (Paris: Flammarion, 1984)
MMHS	Colette, *My Mother's House and Sido*, trans. Una Vincenzo Troubridge and Enid McLeod (Harmondsworth: Penguin, 1966)
NWJ	Nicole Ward Jouve, *Colette* (Brighton: Harvester Press, 1987)
SF	Thurman, *Secrets of the Flesh: A Life of Colette* (London: Bloomsbury Publishing, 1999)
SVV	Colette, Sido, suivi de Les Vrilles de la Vigne (Paris: Livre de Poche, Fayard/Hachette, 2004)
TP	Colette, 'Le Patriarche', in *Bella-Vista* (Paris: J. Ferenczi et fils, 1937); 'The Patriarch', in *The Rainy Moon*.
TRM	Colette, *The Rainy Moon and Other Stories*, trans. Antonia White (Harmondsworth, Penguin, 1976)

NOTE ON THE TEXT

Colette's published literary output was prodigious. For this book, I have concentrated on just four texts that were key for me. I have made my own translations of Colette's work throughout, specifically for this project.

References to Colette's work are to the particular editions of the books I have been consulting rather than to first editions thereof. When I translate her words, I give a reference not only to her original French text in the particular edition from which I have been working, but also to a published English version, so that readers unfamiliar with French can look up relevant passages, if they want to, in an easily available edition. When I translate from French texts not available in English translation, I just give the reference to the French edition I have been using.

The Bibliography does not pretend to be exhaustive. I list only the works by Colette that are the subject of this book, plus other works by her from which I quote or which I mention in passing. References are to the particular French editions of works I have been consulting, with their dates of publication, rather than to first editions. Dates of first publication are given in brackets in the main text when I mention particular works. I list relevant titles in English translation where appropriate.

INTRODUCTION

Rereading Colette

Colette has been a literary mother to me. Her work has fed, nurtured, and inspired me both as a reader and as a writer, and continues to delight me. Reading involves entering a conversation with a book. Writing back to Colette continues our conversation.

I could choose my literary mother. Our relationship existed in parallel with the one I had with my actual mother, Monique. She was French, matriarchal, Catholic, undemonstrative. When I was a young woman, wrestling with her powerful intellectual and moral influence, I needed to assert my difference from her, to struggle for freedom and independence. I turned my back on the canonical writers she valued, mainly pre-twentieth-century ones such as Molière, and searched for others. I remember admiring novels such as *L'Astragale* (1965) by Albertine Sarrazin, for example, *La Bâtarde* (1964) by Violette Leduc, *L'Amant* (1984) by Marguerite Duras, which all, in their own ways, concerned young women battling convention.

When eventually I discovered Colette's writing, I entered an enticing landscape distinguished by its straightforwardly amoral celebration of sensuality, the materiality of food and plants and creatures. Bodies and appetites were examined and cherished precisely for what they were. The Catholicism in which I had grown up was more contradictory, depending on the sensual effects of music, paintings, incense, and costumes to lure and hold the faithful, while at the same time preaching emotional and sexual repression. I was always searching for ecstasy, and as a teenager found it both in church and in the library. Once I left home, the library won. I stopped believing in God and going to Mass and stepped up my reading. The struggle against priestly authority came at a certain cost: knowing I had wounded my mother. Catholicism had formed her, was to be trusted and followed. Back in France, Catholicism was ordinary and basic; a bedrock of truth taken for granted; not discussed. In England, it made my mother stand out. Why did her religion matter so much to her? Partly, I think, because it had shaped her growing up, loving and obeying her parents, partly because it underlined her French identity as an immigrant to the UK who tried to integrate yet also needed to assert her difference, partly because it supported her power in the family. In my childish eyes she represented the Virgin Mary, that combination of adorable queen meant to shelter and protect you, and scary policewoman instructed by the male-dominated Church to control you. Repudiating my mother's religion, I repudiated her, it seemed. When I attacked the Church for misogyny, I was attacking her. I felt guilty, caught in a muddle of needing to rebel against her while still wanting to be accepted. I envied Colette's female characters, who did not seem to suffer from such conflicts. Colette showed women as indifferent to religious rules, enjoying many different forms of pleasure, making up their own methods of survival, and not feeling guilty.

As a teenager, I had had a certain resistance to reading Colette. I had been taken in by the prevalent image of her in British culture as the exponent of would-be 'naughty', frou-frou archness, an imported image exemplified in *Gigi*, the film of her eponymous novel (1945), with Maurice Chevalier coyly growling 'Thank Heaven for Little Girrrls', oozing twinkly-eyed charm. Watching the film, I felt baffled and uneasy, but could not spell out why. When I read *Gigi* in my early twenties, the story of a girl being groomed for upmarket prostitution disturbed me by its matter-of-factness. This is how it is, the novel seemed to be saying: but with luck, you will be rescued by marriage to a rich man. I could not find words to express my disquiet, and fell back on self-criticism, concluding I was prudish.

I felt similarly awkward reading *Claudine at School* (1900), Colette's novel written for her husband Henry Gauthier-Villars, the man-about-town and journalist nicknamed Willy who ran a factory of literary ghost-hacks, recounting teenage goings-on in a country village classroom. Its hints of lesbianism, inserted at Willy's insistence, were smutty and cynical. They scared me, given that I loved my girlfriends, fell in love with female teachers, and knew that in the Catholic culture in which I had grown up lesbianism was seen as disgusting and wicked.

Colette's work was canonical in France but not in England. My French A and S Levels involved my reading only male authors. My English Literature degree did involve reading French female writers, but only premodern ones such as Marie de France and Christine de Pisan. Did my mother, who taught French, read Colette? I do not think so. She rarely spoke of modern writers. After her death, when I took away some of her books, I discovered that she had possessed all Simone de Beauvoir's memoirs. She had not mentioned reading them. Part of mourning my mother involved regretting having so often avoided discussing French literature with her. I deprived both of us of the pleasure we might have had in such conversations.

In 1979 the recently founded The Women's Press published Colette's *La Naissance du Jour* (1928) as *Break of Day,* in Enid McLeod's 1961 translation. A feminist press promoting Colette as an important writer for modern readers made me see her afresh, understand her differently. *Break of Day* was a good book with which to begin that process. It resists categorization, appearing at one moment to be a novel, at another part of an autobiography, at another a prose poem musing on ageing, love, sex, and the mother-daughter bond, at another a how-to manual for gardening and entertaining in the summer heat of Provence, at yet another a series of sketches of friends, lovers, pets. The whole thing is held together by Colette's style, which is racy, salty, sharp, epigrammatic, poetic.

I began to read all the fiction by Colette I came across. Later, I learned that Colette wrote not only novels but also journalism, plays, memoirs, an opera libretto, film scripts, theatre and music and literary criticism, short stories, advertising leaflets, and letters. In the 1980s I stuck to the fiction.

Colette's writing explored and reinvented form. Her books crucially suggested that you could mix fiction and memoir, fiction and autobiography, translating one into the other and back again and producing something new. Like cake mixture transformed by going into the oven. That willingness to draw on her own experience seemed revolutionary, for in the 1980s one way to condemn autobiographical fiction by women was to dismiss it as merely confessional, not properly grown-up, masculine, and imaginative, but limited, garrulous, and turgid.

Confessional? There was a big difference, for me, between the kind of confession I had endured as a child, the abject penitent confessing to the powerful priest, one-to-one in the confessional, and begging for forgiveness, and the kind of disclosures groups of feminists were making to one another as equals in consciousness-raising sessions. (Perhaps I should say trying to make, for I remember how difficult it felt to speak certain of my truths, how tempted I felt to gloss over those difficulties, simply be glib.) As a beginner writer, I learned, from my first experiments writing short stories, that writing realist fiction confined me. It seemed to stay on the surface of events. I wanted to dig deeper down, gain access to my unconscious imagination. At the same time, I did not want to write stream of consciousness. I tackled these problems of form and shape when writing my first novel, *A Piece of the Night* (1978). This was autobiographical in that it concerned a contemporary ex-Catholic character, partly based on myself, struggling against Church and parental authorities, but it also invented a whole other story set in the imperialist past in order to make sense of the patriarchal present, and drew on images from the unconscious and from dreams. It was hard to validate my kind of writing, which lacked the irony and cool so valued in those days.

Reading Colette taught me that there existed a wealth of ways to use autobiographical material. She seemed able to break through taboos and rules about literary behaviour, female behaviour, and invent new forms to express her new content. She encouraged me to invent my own new forms.

I was trying to explore female subjectivity, both speakable and unspeakable. Colette wrote about this brilliantly, dryly,

5

lovingly, mockingly. I learned from reading her that you could simultaneously be a woman (albeit a troubled one) and also a writer, an intellectual; the categories were not in conflict. She just got on with it and so should I. That was my mother's cry whenever I mentioned difficulties in living and wanted to discuss them: just get on with it! I can value that advice now, but could not then.

I grew up in a culture that named and divided Writers and Women Writers. Male writers were the norm. They concealed their sex in full sight and were assumed to have universal appeal. Female writers were Othered; sexed and particular. Male literary journalists constantly praised a small pantheon of white middle-class male writers, seen as geniuses, a status that excluded women. Writing by women, both black and white, could be patronized as nice, as quirky, was simultaneously considered second rate, not worthy of male attention. A few exceptions proved the rule.

However, in the feminist culture of the 1970s and 1980s, women's writing—that is to say, women authors asserting the history and culture associated with sexual difference—briefly became a radical, subversive category. Following the debates around femaleness and femininity initiated by French writers such as Helene Cixous, Julia Kristeva, and Catherine Clément, extracts from whose work I read in English in the early 1980s,[1] it became possible to aspire to telling new, unsettling truths, even as these required fictional art for their embodiment. Colette seemed to have got there way back. She portrayed femininity as a performance or a disguise or a fancy-dress costume, rather than claiming it as innate and essential; she wrote about the female body and its complicated feelings, relationships between women, maternal power and ambivalence, female abjection and cruelty and desire. Exploring these subjects, she necessarily also explored maleness and masculinity, in novels such as *Chéri* (1920) and *La Fin de Chéri* (*The End of Chéri*) (1926). I felt encouraged by her examination of these themes and subjects. She gave me permission to do likewise.

My childhood combined contradictory elements: the obedience inculcated at home and at school mixed with a fair amount of physical freedom, lack of adult supervision. I remember, in England, enjoying rowdy playground games, playing outdoors in the brambly wildernesses of local parks and the woods abutting our neighbourhood, roller-skating around the local streets, jumping between the roofs of old bomb shelters, running home at night in the dark, and in France spending long afternoons swimming at Etretat, exploring the rocks and pools, the caves under the cliffs. I knew I was a girl but that hardly mattered. Puberty arriving when I was 10 was a shock, signing me as female in a way that felt limiting and repressive. Primary school had been mixed; boys and girls could be friends; I relished that mixing as well as having a female best friend. In single-sex convent secondary school, Catholic training now kicked in. It instilled a distrust of the body and its appetites, self-hatred as a woman, the sense that body was in conflict with spirit, the latter superior to the former. Getting clear of this damage took years. Reading Colette, I began to see that you could think differently, that you could write your way into, around, and through these damaging conflicts, and experience sensual joy—*la jouissance*—in the process. Kristeva talked of the *jouissance* of reading, but it is there in writing too. I thank Colette for what she has given and taught me.

Writing this book I hope to explore those gifts and teachings in the light of how they appear to me today. I shall reread certain texts by Colette that were key for me in the past, both fiction and memoir, to see what they say to me now, to discover in what way my reading of them, my understanding of them, may have changed or been enriched or replaced by others. I look back at those key works of Colette with an understanding mediated by the biographies and critical works I have read in the interim, in particular the biographies by Michèle Sarde (1978), Claude Francis and Fernande Gontier (1997), and Judith Thurman (1999), and the studies by Nicole Ward Jouve (1987) and by Julia Kristeva (2002). Some I read as soon as they appeared; others more recently (I have hardly dipped a toe into Kristeva's book yet but mean to do so …). Looked at together, they compose a Cubist-style portrait of Colette, sharp with clash and contradiction. Individually, they offer intriguingly different perspectives. Francis and Gontier reveal new research shattering old myths. Michele Sarde is tender and affectionate where Judith Thurman is tart. Nicole Ward Jouve concentrates on language. And so on.

In her lifetime Colette was read and appreciated by the general book-loving public. The literary critics took a while to catch up with popular opinion. She ended up a literary *grande dame*, showered with honours, given a state funeral, but in the beginning she had to fight even to establish her authorship of her own work. Her husband Willy signed her Claudine novels as his own. First of all she came out as Colette Willy and then, simply, as Colette.

This soubriquet seems to have first been given her by Willy, who referred to her, in a letter to a male friend, as his pretty little Colette (SF 58). It sounds like a feminine diminutive form, along the lines of *soubrette, midinette, pierrette*. In fact, it is a masculine name, her father Jules Colette's surname. Her use of this name mingling masculine and feminine identities was appropriate: in the age of the Belle Epoque and its ambivalent relish of exaggerated femininity, Colette took pride in what she saw as her own virility. Her novels characteristically both underline and undermine gendered conventions concerning sex and love. In an age obsessed with women as sexual objects, Colette wrote about them as sexual subjects. Her girls and young women are sexually curious and daring. For example, teenaged Vinca in *Le Blé en herbe* (*Green Wheat*) (1923) treats her first sexual encounter with a boy with panache. The following morning he indulges in a long, solemn bout of self-questioning, then spots her pottering on her balcony. Rather than looking overwhelmed by what he takes to have been a life-changing event for a trembling virgin, she is shaking out her hair, watering her potted fuchsia, singing cheerfully.

I first wrote about Colette in a short story, 'Colette Looks Back', which was published in my collection *Mud: Stories of Sex and Love* (2010). For some time I had been making fictional portraits of male writers, playing with their biographies and inventing alternative versions or filling in perceived gaps, in order to spotlight overlooked but (to me) significant women in their lives. Sometimes I made composite pictures of these writers—for example, merging aspects of Flaubert and Mallarmé in *The Looking Glass* (2000)—and sometimes I disguised well-known individuals—for example, William Wordsworth and his French lover Annette Vallon in *Fair Exchange* (1999). This tampering with received truths developed out of my earlier interest in hagiography. As a Catholic child I had been fascinated by the lives of the saints that I read at convent school, the miracles and heroism involved. The medieval collection *The Golden Legend*'s tales of virgin martyrs being raped

and tortured might appeal to the masochistic sensibility inculcated as part of Catholic femininity but also, as Marina Warner
has pointed out, at least provided stories of female courage and
daring (*FBB, passim*). I wrote my novel *Impossible Saints* (1997) as a
riposte to *The Golden Legend*, as a way of exploring/inventing the
secret life of Teresa of Avila and other women saints, also as a
way of resisting Catholic teaching. My love of reading biographies
of writers followed on from my love of reading saints' lives. It
enabled me to set up my own pantheon of writers. 'Colette Looks
Back' functioned as a love letter to Colette and also let me invent
a premarital erotic episode for her. This also formed a fictional
mask for reimagining and recounting an erotic episode in my
own life. Desire, falling in love, often fires my writing. Colette
embodies a heady example of how that can continue well into old
age.

Writing about Colette in fictional guise felt un-anxious and free.
Writing this current book feels far more nerve-racking. All those
old super-critical ghosts from childhood and from my education
raise their heads and come prowling to snap at my ankles. My
mother (a particular image of her, at any rate) was always at the
head of the pack. Now I address my mother's ghost: did you in
fact read Colette's work and not talk about it with me because I
rejected your views on most things for so long? Did you simply
assume I was not interested in hearing what you had to say? Who
could blame you if you did! What did you think of Colette's books
if indeed you read them? In the last years of Mum's life we would
eat supper together by candlelight, relishing French food and
wine, enjoying talking to each other, listening to each other. After
my father died, she needed a new sparring partner, and I took on
the role. Sometimes I would talk to her in French, and she loved

that. How often when younger I would not give her that pleasure! Yes, as a young woman speaking only in English, I was certainly acting out my rebellion against my mother tongue. Also, I now think, I was simplifying my confusion over my identity. With one parent French, middle class, and Catholic, and the other English, working class, and Protestant, I did not know where I belonged. Could I identify with both parents? What about maleness and femaleness? What about being a twin? Unable to integrate all these strands of inheritance, in my early twenties I tried to ignore them. At any rate, I first read Colette's work in English, and continued doing so. Now, as I read her in French, as I make my own translations for the paragraphs I want to quote, I think of my mother, quick with an opinion, answering back, sometimes smiling, insisting on her own point of view. I am reading with my mother in mind. I am in conversation with her as I am with Colette.

My opening chapter, as you will see, is much longer than the three following it. At the time of writing, this felt intuitively right. In it, I explore just one book, which seemed to demand to be treated at length. I give myself plenty of time to explore the importance of childhood in a writer's development, and why the figure of the mother matters to Colette so much. That figure, differently viewed, is central to the works I have chosen to reread and to write about in the much shorter chapters that follow.

I hope that in reassessing Colette through rereading her, I can make contact with other readers who may become inspired to reread her also. Perhaps this book can become a bridge into Colette country for readers approaching her for the first time.

1

MOTHER HOUSE

How to begin? It is obvious. Begin at the beginning. With the mother. Both remembered and imagined. Remembering and imagining are connected energies. Memory is the mother of the Muses. In Colette's work the mother appears as a figure of powerful, overarching mythic status who is also a local, particular goddess.

Colette, placing the image of the mother at the centre of her texts, was revolutionary in her own day, and still seems so to me a hundred years later. Her inspiration came from her own mother, Adèle-Eugénie-Sidonie Landoy, whom she sometimes addresses as Sido, the name given to his wife by her adoring second husband, Colette's father, and sometimes simply calls *ma mère*.

I want to reflect on my rereading of two works concerning Sido. The first is *La Maison de Claudine* (1922).

I do not remember precisely when I first read it. Sometime in my late twenties or early thirties, probably. If I bought a copy, I have lost it. In those days I kept having to dispose of my collections of books, as my insecure and poverty-stricken life as a freelance writer meant that I moved frequently and could not take trunkfuls of books with me to the assortment of bedsits I perched in. At some point I rebought certain texts by Colette, including *La Maison de Claudine*. I still possess that Penguin Modern Classics copy, a 1988 reprint, featuring Roger Senhouse's 1953 translation. This deploys the title *My Mother's House*. Senhouse explains, in his introduction, that the original French title, referencing the (earlier) Claudine series of novels, was probably used for publicity purposes, to imply that this new work is similarly fiction and that it features Colette's young heroine Claudine. Not so, Senhouse says. This is strictly memoir (*LMC* 123; *MMHS* 117).

Certainly, the house of this book's title is Sido's. She is the presiding spirit of the interior. Houses are traditionally images of maternal bodies; caves of making. Michèle Sarde links house to womb: 'an active place, the site of gestation and production' (*CFF* 36). Colette's book is the house, is the maternal body, is Sido, is the shrine of memory that the daughter designs and builds.

La Maison de Claudine collects certain of Colette's memories. From my first reading, so long ago, I retain an impression of the book's sensual evocation of home and village life, a childhood rich in liberty, adventures pursued outdoors. I have reread it partly because I had forgotten so much of it, partly because I was feeling newly curious about Colette's early life, and mainly because it depicts the mother-daughter relationship. Usually this is foregrounded. At other moments it forms a background—for example, to anecdotes concerning Colette's two brothers.

La Maison de Claudine is a short book. Colette did not write long ones! Its compactness and compression help give it power. It is composed as a series of vignettes, a kaleidoscope of bright, flashing scenes featuring Sido. In one four-page anecdote, 'Le Rire' ('Laughter'), she is shown laughing, on the day of her beloved husband's funeral, at a kitten's antics. In another, 'La Petite Bouilloux' ('The Little Bouilloux Girl'), equally brief, she scolds her little daughter for wanting fancy, glitzy clothes. These accounts resemble snapshots, taken from different angles, mainly close-ups, then arranged in narrative order. On the one hand that order seems randomly organized and on the other carefully so. The form of *La Maison de Claudine* defies conventional classification. It appears to be a memoir, but it also reads like a collection of linked short stories. These prose pieces, written as fragments, each one a miniature complete in itself, separate from the others, simultaneously connect to each other, across the gaps between them. They give an effect of having risen up randomly, moments of life that feel both transient and important. They can simply be enjoyed for what they are, captured lightly like seedheads or soap bubbles, held balanced on an open palm before they vanish. At the same time they can be given meaning. Actually, I cannot define the form of this book. It is itself; Colette's invention.

Did she like taking photos? Which side of the camera did she prefer to be on? Certainly she seems to have enjoyed posing for photographs, whether coy, winsome ones advertising her Claudine books, or sexy publicity stills for her music-hall performances, or group portraits with family and friends, or carefully composed studies of herself plus daughter, child, dog, servant. Did her involvement with photography influence her development of a literary form? If her narrative's rapid succession of images reminds me of a shutter flash and click, and a stream of photos being produced, it also reminds me of a child and mother playing hide and seek: blink, open your eyes, hide your eyes, blink, the mother hides, look, she's back. *Fort-da* on both sides. Sido is not easy to catch: she is sound, movement, echo, shadow. Not some static Madonna posed seated on a stool or a throne, but an active, darting being often glimpsed escaping from the house rather than belonging in it. Part of the garden, and of the work going on there. Queen of a queendom embracing both inside and outside.

The effect of the book, once read, is to suggest simultaneously a whole, sparkling ball of images, seen all at once in a single glance, like an abstract painting, existing in an eternal moment of now, and an unravelled, unwound narrative existing in time. A fruitful tension exists between its effect of collage, torn bits flung about and captured in a pattern, and its smoothly unspooling narrative. We are alerted to the process of making something with words: the writer puts some words in and takes others out. This may sound obvious and banal, but it is not. It refers to the struggle of writing, how that leaves its traces in the text. Colette's prose is not like the clear glass of a windowpane that you look through and do not notice as you survey the world it reveals. In Colette, the glass is part of the material. She wields the lens and reminds us she is doing so.

Colette wrote this book long after she had left home aged 18, when she married Willy and moved to Paris. She is looking back nostalgically at a lost, beloved time and place and person. Her nostalgia involves her search for origins, both literary and familial. She tracks both by focusing her gaze on her search for her mother.

The word nostalgia derives from *nostos*, meaning home, and *algos*, meaning pain. It used to be seen as a specific form of neurosis afflicting a particular group of sufferers, which involved depression and longing, an insistent desire to dwell psychologically in the past that hindered capable living in the present. Nowadays that precise definition has been softened and broadened. Nostalgia has come to refer to a widespread and tolerated hankering after comfort and security, obtained by dwelling on valued aspects of the past that need to be recuperated, in both the private and the public spheres. For example, people may regret certain beneficial traditions, labour relations, solidarity and community spirit that seem to be lost in modern culture and, if restored, would help to cure the damaged present.

Nostalgia's critics link it to sentimentality and frown upon it as reactionary and dangerous, pointing out that in political discourse it may help rewrite the past in dishonest ways, in order to obliterate episodes of domination and exploitation. On the level of literature, is Colette's cherishing of nature and rural customs nostalgic in a negative way, given that it does not emphasize the poverty and hardships endured by the farmworkers in her parents' village?

Nostalgia for one's maternal landscape can similarly be viewed with suspicion, though this may be less true nowadays than it was in the 1970s, when I began reading Colette's work. In those days, mothers were meant to be left behind, so ran the conventional wisdom, particularly by sons. Mothers might give birth and milk, forming then nurturing a child physically, and inculcate beginner's morals, but their ultimate job was to prepare a child to leave them. Their influence might endure at a personal level, fondly invoked, but was not talked about publicly as of intellectual importance.

I link this traditional idea of a mother's role to the stern, commonsensical, simplistic narrative concerning literature that was around in my early twenties, which I picked up from book reviews. This instructed us that male writers were gods riding solo, making something out of nothing, admitting no anxiety-inducing influence. Male writers in interview did not discuss women writers and conveyed the impression that their books were certainly not born of reading them.

This seemed linked to the cultural necessity in those days for heterosexual men to be as unlike women as possible, to deny anything 'feminine' in themselves. Men had to separate from their mothers, kill them psychologically if necessary, set their faces to look forward not back. Rare was the heterosexual male writer who admitted his mother as a major inspiration for his work. A woman writer who did so would be met with shrugs. Feminist writers might be discussing their identities as rebellious daughters, as struggling mothers, but could be dismissed as hysterics.

Colette, disregarding the heroic male model of creation, becomes intriguingly radical. Her nostalgia involves her breaking the taboo on citing the mother as inspirational. She searches for and finds the mother and brings her centre stage.

Colette's veneration of Sido is both straightforward and complicated, occasionally betrays itself as veiling tricky episodes. Perhaps leaving out certain events. Colette insists she looks back at a happy childhood, yet possible omissions are hinted at by her giving us her story in this form of fragments, of separate, assembled memories—that is to say, vignettes composed by herself, a mature artist. She is in control of her material, and yet the book gives me a sense of powerful undercurrents tugging against the carefully directed flow of language, as if unconscious energies are somehow at play. Colette allows me to speculate about that by leaving gaps between her vignettes. I can enter these gaps, guess at and invent what may be hiding there. The sexual double standard, for a start. The unhappiness it inflicts. For example, the piece called

'La "Fille de mon Père'" ('The "Daughter of my Father"'), concerning Sido's tale of her father's marital infidelities and her jealousy of her little half-sister, is followed by 'La Noce' ('The Wedding') concerning Sido's opinions of an unmarried pregnant housemaid and a swaggering village bride. The juxtaposition of the two pieces, the jump across between them, suggests a writerly free association, linking the tales' subjects, on Colette's part, while the white gap separating them suggests her acknowledgement that in Sido's village certain things cannot be spelt out. Colette, our narrator, is a listener, a witness, a child struggling to connect her own knowledge of animals giving birth to grown-up hypocrisies around sexual morality. What is going on in the heavy silences surrounding certain subjects? She invites me to collaborate with her. She makes me think about the primary meanings of words such as memory and forgetting and childhood and myth.

The Christian myth that shaped European culture for so long begins with human beings inhabiting paradise, the Garden of Eden. If a happy childhood is a paradise, then as we grow up it necessarily becomes a paradise lost, so runs conventional wisdom. We supposedly look back on childhood as something that is over, gone forever. Colette shows us, however, that childhood keeps springing up inside us, refound and renewed and reinvented. The maternal house is not lost. Memory not only preserves things but brings them back alive. The past becomes the present. A resurrection. A magical conjuring.

This is made possible through writing; through Colette's wizardry as a writer. She writes as a heretic. For her, it is not just childhood that is paradise but the maternal body itself and the child's relationship to it. Conventionally, in the west, women were lined up with body and nature, and men with mind and culture; men did things to nature and created culture. In Colette's revolutionary version, the mother is identified with nature but also with culture; the two fuse. Sido personifies the radiant garden and at the same time its speech. It can be no accident that Sido is positioned in *La Maison de Claudine* as a creator of meaning, a mentor of reading, a judge of others' stories, whether her small daughter's, as she tries to wriggle out of trouble, or those found in books. The writer's mother is shown throughout as herself a teller of tales, an inventor of myths, a juggler with words. Colette paints a distinctive, particular portrait that layers linguistic effects across visual ones: the sounds of Sido's voice, her call, the turns of her phrases, her relish of spoken unconventional opinions, of salty orally delivered anecdotes, coexist with glimpsed images of interiors, street corners, back gardens.

Rereading *La Maison de Claudine*, I now see it as distinguished by being a work preoccupied with narrative form, and in particular with those forms encountered in its author's childhood: oral storytelling, myths, and fairy tales. These, the book demonstrates, continue to be valued by the adult writer as a way of re-creating that childhood and giving shape to its experiences, both pleasurable and painful. I understand them, now, as crucial to Colette's composing of Sido's portrait. I did not notice them before, though they were hiding in plain sight.

The family house in Saint-Sauveur contained a library rich in both fiction and non-fiction. Colette, educated at the village public school, supplemented its narrowly focused teaching by exploring the books amassed by her parents. For the child, books were sensual; fingertip friends; their identities created and discovered anew through the colour, shape, and touch of their spines. She could pick out her favourites in the dark; familiar, beloved bodies she caressed.

The vignette 'Ma Mère et les livres' ('My Mother and the Books') sketches the mother–daughter relationship through its account of the mother's and daughter's reading. Sido regularly reread her collection of the eighteen volumes of Saint-Simon's works, keeping them one at a time on her bedside table, and prescribing them to the uncomprehending 8 year old. Earlier, as a small child, Colette enjoyed flicking through the pages of Perrault's fairy tales. In 'Ma Mère et les livres' she remembers 'adoring the princess in her chariot, dreamy under an elongated crescent moon, and Beauty asleep in the woods, and being smitten by Puss in Boots' (*LMC* 36; *MMHS* 48) and relished the illustrations to these tales by Walter Crane. Later on in her childhood she read novels by Alphonse Daudet, Prosper Mérimée, and Victor Hugo. She disdained *The Three Musketeers*, by Alexandre Dumas, urged on her by her parents, but did read his story *The Queen's Necklace*, which gleamed through her dreams several nights running.

Looking back on herself as that girl rummaging through the fiction writers on her parents' bookshelves, Colette remembers discovering how they concentrated to a great extent on love, and how her mother offered a lens through which to view them:

I learned from them, long before I was old enough to fall in love, that love is complicated and tyrannical and even burdensome, since my mother quibbled at the prominence they gave it. 'It's really embarrassing, the amount of love in these books,' she would say. 'In life, my poor Minet-Chéri, people have other fish to fry. All these lovers you see in books, haven't they ever had children to bring up or gardens to tend? Minet-Chéri, be my judge: have you or your brothers ever heard me harping on about love like people do in books? And yet it seems to me I could demand a chapter of my own; I've had two husbands and four children!' (*LMC* 37; *MMHS* 49)

Sido becomes the child Colette's literary mentor. She tells her to read what she likes and just be sensible, to keep it to herself if she understands 'too much ... perhaps there's no such thing as a harmful book'. When little Colette teeters at the edge of 'fascinating abysses of terror' teeming with phantoms, wizards, shadowy evil beasts, Sido is at hand, with her wise, 'magical counsel' not to let these monsters climb up her daughter's 'dangling plaits' (*LMC* 38; *MMHS* 49).

I read a fairy-tale hint here, a reference to Rapunzel. Rapunzel's mother, overfond and overprotective, locked up her daughter in a tower and then left her alone, not realizing that Rapunzel's long hair, let down out of the window, could facilitate entry by eager princes, monstrous only in a possessive mother's eyes. Sido will behave differently, it seems. Instead of imprisoning then neglecting her beloved child, she will stand watchfully beside her and offer an opinion. Colette learned early on to develop her own literary taste, to trust her own stubborn insistence on preferring one text to another. However, it is thanks to Sido's robust commentaries, perhaps, that Colette is able to recognize that gift of her mother's:

I don't know what literary coldness, healthy on the whole, kept me from romantic delirium, and made me—a little later, when I tackled books whose fabled power seemed infallible—capable of criticizing them rather than falling victim to them. Was I still, in this regard, imitating my mother, whose distinctive ingenuousness inclined her to deny evil, even though her curiosity made her seek it out and contemplate it, mixed up with the good, with wondering eyes? (*LMC* 38; *MMHS* 49)

Sido mothered Colette into being able to become a writer who would do just that, look at evil mixed up with good. Colette once wrote, in a letter to her friend Renée Hamon, who had asked her for advice on writing: 'Look for a long time at what pleases you, and for even longer at what displeases you.'[1] I think she learned that from Sido. Colette's biographers Claude Francis and Fernande Gontier point to Sido's embrace of Fourieresque philosophy as a young woman:

> the passions, Fourier said, are 'the mistresses of the world' but our civilization condemns them under the name of mortal sins and vices. But the repression of passion is the origin of the evils, crimes and pathological problems of civilized societies. Rather than repress them, Fourier proposed integrating them … transforming them into beneficial forces … Sido soaked up these theories. 'Evil and good, she would say, may be equally splendid and fertile.' (FG 22)

Sido seems to have been able both to contain acknowledgement of the 'heat' exemplified by the passions and the 'coldness' required for their dispassionate examination in literature, and to have wanted to pass this wise acceptance on to her daughter. Looking for a long time at what society would call displeasing, indeed immoral, she allowed herself a certain ambivalence. Colette gives an example of this in an apparently autobiographical short story 'Le Patriarche' ('The Patriarch'), which I first read in Antonia White's translation.[2] Sido's son Achille, as a young doctor, attends a young woman giving birth in a local cottage.

She is only 14, still a child herself. She has three sisters. Achille realizes, from the farmer father's swagger and boastful hints, that the latter sleeps with his four daughters and sires their babies. Sido both deprecates the story and admires the beauty of the children. One day she spots one of the daughters sitting on the cottage doorstep, suckling her baby. The situation may be 'abominable', but the long-eyelashed infant is 'enchanting'. Sido muses to Colette, aged 15, on the 'ancient patriarchs …'. The narrative's row of dots invites the reader to imagine these gentlemen's sexual habits. Sido says 'after all …', perhaps accepting their entitlement, but then falls silent (TP 131). The cottage appears to be isolated, ethically if not physically, outside the village and its moral and legal frameworks, unseen by the arbiters of religion and customs. Sido's version of events, framed by Colette, gives it a fairy-tale quality. The scene feels dreamy, pastoral, belonging in an Eden where sin has not yet been invented. Outside history.

In *From the Beast to the Blonde*, Marina Warner writes compellingly of how fairy tales transmit less archetypal truths, as Jungian interpreters claim, than problems in real-life families (*FBB, passim*). She points to how father–daughter incest is explored and contained in a traditional story such as 'Donkeyskin'. I first encountered incest as a reality (that is to say, as a story) when, in 1993, I bought my house in the north-western French countryside and moved to live there with my husband Jim. We discovered from a neighbour that the previous owner had sexually abused his daughters. He and his wife no longer got on, and she had moved to sleep downstairs, leaving him in the attic, his bed divided from his daughters' just by a curtain. One of the daughters had escaped one night and sought refuge with my neighbour. Escaping prosecution because of his weak health, subsequently shunned in the district, the father was selling up. Later I discovered, from other stories told by my neighbour, that sexual abuse had been common among farming families living on these isolated farms outside the village. The man living near the watermill just down the lane from us had similarly abused his daughters after his wife died. Shame kept people quiet. Male power and privilege were protected by the Catholic Church as well as by the state. Nostalgia for the old ways of mutual help and support, which my neighbours were fond of recalling, brushed over these examples of rape and exploitation, which did not fit the accepted narrative of benevolence.

I remember how on my first reading of Sido's semi-admiration for the incest, for the beautiful babies it produced, I felt enraged on the daughters' behalf. The father had raped them and that was that. Sido, I thought, was romanticizing. Prettifying. She seemed to be implying that the daughters were complicit. How could they be? What choice did they have? Sido's attitude not only angered me but made me uneasy, made me remember how I had been a little girl who adored her dad. What had my fantasies been? I felt that my newly bought little house was tainted not only by the facts of the previous owner's abuse of his daughters but also by childhood fears stirring inside myself. I dealt with the turmoil by writing a story, 'No Hands' (in my short story collection *Playing Sardines* (2001)), which drew on the fairy tale of the maiden with no hands.

The Greek myths are full of stories about incest and rape, sometimes glossed over by kindlier names. Did Colette as a child ever read a collection of Greek myths? She does not say so. Yet, as well as fairy tale, whose locus is earth, *La Maison de Claudine* seems to me to employ myth, whose characters move between Olympus (the heaven-mountain) and earth. Sido appears in Colette's work as a goddess, as various critics and biographers have pointed out. It is an obvious inference to draw.

Nowadays, in western consumer culture, the word goddess has been banalized, referring cynically or ironically to celebrities making money out of the unpaid traditionally female work of cooking and running a household. Their followers can achieve similar status by buying a new cookery book, a new guide to decluttering, a new dress or lipstick. These goddesses may inspire envy, drive the need to spend money and consume commodities, but they do not provoke terror and awe as their predecessors did. The Greek and Roman goddesses I encountered in books read in childhood could make forests tremble, could ride thunderstorms. They were certainly capable, when insufficiently revered, of dealing out punishments, taking revenge. Sido, in Colette's images, retains the ancient power and wiliness of those pre-Christian goddesses. In her daughter's eyes she is the centre of the world, the foundation of life. She is the source of meaning, but also of equivocation and contradiction, the arbiter of morals but also of ways to escape them.

In Christian terms, Sido's importance is, of course, heretical. In the traditional Catholic culture of France, to which Colette was exposed through catechism classes at the village church, God was spoken of as He. The God of the Old Testament was sternly, necessarily male. When in the New Testament God decided to incarnate himself as his son Jesus, the latter's mother Mary, though a god-bearer, was less than a god, merely a human vessel. She had nothing to do with creating her divine son; she merely contained him. Like Colette, I learned this dogma in childhood. Modern Catholic theology still holds to it.

As a young woman I relished the opposing, feminist view, which argued that male patriarchs merely invented a theology of women to suit themselves. Sweetly telling women they had a special, holy feminine role and place as helpmeets and mothers, they could deny women's sexual power and agency. Over the years I have developed my current view: the Fall is a shorthand for our understanding that we are mortal, subject to the laws of nature, the facts of sex and death. Catholicism resists this knowledge, twists it around, asserts that Eve's disobedience, her curiosity, resulted in the Fall; therefore women, susceptible to the lures of the serpent, are to blame for it. We are born of woman and later on we die, and so, runs the patriarchal logic of the early Fathers of the Church, death is women's fault. Jesus triumphs over death by defying natural laws and being resurrected, and so original sin (the fact of having been born imperfect, born of faulty, disobedient woman) is redeemed. As a woman, Mary cannot be directly connected to the divine. Her consolation prize is to be regarded as a perfected woman, because her maternity is sexless (she remains a virgin) and because, as a god-bearer, she has become regarded, according to the doctrine of the Immaculate Conception, as lacking original sin.

What is repressed returns. Popular culture in Europe, perhaps with some deep archaic sense of continuity remembering Mary as the goddess Artemis, seems to resist Catholicism's demeaning of Mary and heretically to accord her goddess status, with the power to heal, forgive, and bless. The countryside of France is dotted with shrines to the strong, benevolent Virgin; she guards and rules over the landscape. Wooden crucifixes with statues of Mary set in their niches rear up at crossroads, blessing swerves in direction. Church frescoes and altarpieces allot her a majestic presence. Medieval depictions of the Coronation of the Virgin in heaven show her seated on her throne, on equal terms with her divine son as he crowns her. An onlooker not knowing the theology involved could easily conclude the two form a divine married couple.

Colette bestows a similar elevated status on Sido. This mother, queen of the earth and the garden as well as of the house, can both cherish and punish, reward and reject. We see her forming the child Colette, teaching her manners, affectionately scolding her, pinching her into shape, at the same time allowing her liberty and encouraging her to think for herself. All of Colette's vignettes stress Sido's authority, originality, and unconventionality. These seem to have ensured that Catholicism did not 'take' with Colette, despite her love, as a little girl, of village processions and holy rituals; what I call the folklore of Catholicism. Country pagan lore and country religious lore can overlap. Colette, like Sido, shed those aspects of her religious inheritance she did not need, and reinvented her rural pagan identity as the whim took her.

Sido's family, the Landoys, were involved in trade and industry. Francis and Gontier remind me explicitly, as Colette does not, that the freethinking Sido was also a bourgeoise who delighted in crystal and porcelain, in fine art and books bound in calf. Her disdain of bourgeois morality, they suggest, probably encouraged her disregard of money, her enjoyment of gambling at cards, her accumulation of the debts that added to the ones she inherited and that eventually crushed the family. Some biographers have blamed Jules Colette, her second husband, for mismanaging the family fortunes, but others, more recently, point out that all he did was fail to pay off Sido's debts. As Alain Brunet declares, in his introduction (2004) to *Sido* (1929),[3] another volume of memoir, the fiscal responsibility was rooted in the complex legal arrangements preceding Sido's first marriage. Captain Colette bore no responsibility for these and had no authority to rescue her. Brunet argues that Sido tried to shift the blame onto the adoring husband she referred to in her letters to her daughter as 'ton pauvre papa' ('your poor father'), making out that he was weak and inept.

Sido's disdain of bourgeois morality could only go so far. She could not step outside family structures of thought embodying the double standard. For example, her belief in free love coexisted with her collaborating with her family's silence over her half-sister Irma, whose declared profession was that of dressmaker but who existed in the demi-monde as a kept woman. Francis and Gontier are clear: 'Colette's fascination for courtisans, for kept women, comes from way back, from this mysterious personage whom the Landoys talked about only in veiled terms' (FG 18).

A goddess can use her power for both good and evil. Judith Thurman depicts Sido as an over-powerful mother who dominated her daughter, thus preparing her for a lifetime of struggling with the power relations involved in love affairs. As an adult, Colette vacillated between dominating and being dominated, Thurman asserts. Her view may be corroborated not so much by Colette's own texts, which present Sido as kindly and wellmeaning and are only ever implicitly negative about her, as by a selective reading of Sido's letters, those in which she is explicit about her childrearing methods. For example, Thurman quotes Sido boasting, in a letter to Colette, about controlling her children's emotions and bodies, breaking her children in, like unruly animals, to hygiene and cleanliness. Thurman writes: 'her kittens never soiled the floor, "and all four of you," she told Colette proudly, "were trained to be just as clean. No pooping in your

beds"' (*SF* 23). There is an echo of this busy watchfulness in Colette's later boasting about how she feeds and weighs her adult stepson Bertrand, an imposed intimacy that seems pretty invasive to me. Léa, in *Chéri*, similarly delights in fattening up and weighing the young protégé who will become her lover.

Alain Brunet takes his criticism further. He points out that *Sido*, composed of three chapters recalling in turn Colette's mother, father, and siblings, is named for Sido only: 'Giving the volume only the mother's name is abusive—which is also a way of announcing, from the first word, the title, that Sido was an abusive mother' (*SVV* 20). Stern words! Brunet does distinguish between Sido, 'the heroine of these recollections', and 'Sidonie Colette, née Landoy, the flesh and blood woman who gave birth to one of the greatest writers in our language' (*SVV* 9). As evidence for his harsh view, Brunet points to Colette's observations in the book. He lists Sido's strictness with her children, her acerbic commentaries on her neighbours, her opinions, which had the weight of legal decrees, of ex-communications, her ferocious jealousy of her daughter-in-law, her disdain for her husband.

However, in *La Maison de Claudine*, Sido is presented, at first reading at least, as primarily benevolent, if would-be all-powerful.

Read in a certain way, the opening scene, set around the village house inhabited by the Colette family, certainly shows Sido as hyper-vigilant. (Could Colette be mapping onto Sido received ideas of the Virgin Mary as omniscient surveillance expert?) Sido appears in her particular domain, the garden, hunting for her two sons and two daughters. 'My mother, small and rounded, in those days when age had not yet emaciated her. She … would lift her head and throw her cry into the air: "The children! Where are the children?" Where? Nowhere' (*LMC* 7; *MMHS* 25). Eventually, Sido gives up calling the truants and returns indoors. The children, it turns out, are hiding close by, stretched out along the overhead branches of trees, delighting in maintaining their silence and escaping the maternal scrutiny. Sido wants to chivvy them in to tea; she worries they will not return even for dinner. Her cry forms the main theme of this memory shaped into a story. We see her, as well as hear her, towards its end:

> 'Where are the children?' She would rise up like an over-careful mother-bitch, breathless from her nonstop searching, head lifted to scent the wind. Her white linen over-sleeves showed that she had been kneading the pastry for a galette, or making a pudding with a hot, velvety sauce of jam and rum. If she had been washing the Havanese dog a long blue apron would be tied round her, and sometimes she would be waving a crackling yellow banner of butcher's paper; in that way she was hoping to collect all at the same time her escaped children and her vagabond cats, hungry for raw meat'. (*LMC* 9; *MMHS* 26)

Sido's plants, her garden, similarly require attention, control, and nurture. Colette shows Sido as an expert and attentive gardener, deeply attuned to the soil, to seasons of growth and flowering. She wears a blue satinette dress (the Madonna's colour) and wields a green watering can. She grows roses and annual flowers in the upper garden, tomatoes, peppers, and aubergines in the lower one. She tends the wisteria, the walnut tree, two small fir trees.

Certainly, an earth goddess. This particular portrait of Sido, grounded in her physical reality, her feet-on-the-ground maternal persona, is balanced against other views Colette gives of her, as thinker, as heretic. She does not want to be written into men's stories about women; written off. When little Colette is upset, to the point of fainting in horror, by a graphic scene of childbirth in a novel by Zola, filched from the forbidden shelf in the house library, Sido comforts her:

> 'It's not so terrible, you know, a baby's birth is far from being terrible … You forget the pain you go through really quickly, you'll see. The proof of that is that women forget it, it's only ever men—and was it any of Zola's business?—who write about it.' (LMC 41; MMHS 52)

Sido is similarly independent in her views of religion. Though she cannot be openly rebellious, since to a certain extent she has got to fit into village life in order to survive, she retains her own strongly held opinions. She makes clear to her daughter her dislike of Catholicism's priestly authorities, whose canonical texts define beliefs and prescribe how human beings should behave. The child Colette is being taught her catechism, whose tutelage proceeds via a succession of questions to which there is only one answer—the correct, approved one. Pondering this, Sido concludes that she distrusts the sacrament of confession, imposed as a necessity on the faithful. She dislikes the very idea of disclosing one's inner life to a priest. She rails to Colette's father:

> 'to reveal one's wrongdoing, to state it and then state it again and show it off! It would be better to keep quiet about it, inflict one's own internal punishment. But confession encourages a child to gush, to strip herself intimately, and soon enough there'll be more vanity in her than humility. I assure you! I'm very unhappy! And I'm going right now to tell the *curé* what I think!' (LMC 116; MMHS 110)

I relish Sido's attitude, since my mother sent us off to confession every Saturday evening, and involved us, as I saw it, in shame and humiliation.

Sido returns from her visit complacent. She has not given the priest a piece of her mind, but she has got from him a prized pelargonium cutting and the promise of a honeysuckle one. Colette's father teases her for her evasion, both tactful and cowardly, but it is possible also to read it as her refusal to speak the speech of the Church, preferring her own:

> she was already out of sight, but her voice still reached us, a subtle soprano, fluctuating with the least emotion, a flexible voice, which reached beyond us to spread the news of cherished plants, grafts, rainfall, hatchings; like the voice of an invisible bird foretelling the weather. (LMC 117; MMHS 111)

Sido's confessions are not made to a higher authority but are a form of communing with herself and with equals.

Colette follows this vignette with an account of how the ancient *curé* is subjugated by Sido's voice and by her 'scandalous sincerity'. Attending weekly Mass, she takes her dog with her. To the priest's reproach, she retorts: 'leave my dog at the church door! What are you afraid he'll learn in church?' She performs all the ritual gestures and defends herself against the *curé*'s suspicions:

> 'How do you know … whether I pray or not? I don't know the Pater Noster, that's true, but it doesn't take long to learn, does it? Nor to forget, for that matter. But during Mass, when you oblige us to kneel, I get two or three peaceful moments for thinking about all my concerns. It strikes me that the little one isn't looking too well, and that I ought to fetch up a bottle of Chateau-Larose to put the roses back into her cheeks. That those unhappy Pluviers are going to bring another child into the world without any baby linen unless I get involved. That tomorrow it's the household wash and I'll have to get up at four o'clock'. Lifting his tanned gardener's hand, he stopped her: 'that will do, that will do. I'll count it all as praying'. (LMC 117; MMHS 111)

Sido has forced this male Church authority to accept her own language, her own version of things. Colette describes how Sido devotedly reads Corneille's plays, concealed by a missal-like cover, in her pew. She puts lay stories inside religious ones.

Colette is showing us how she learned strategy from Sido: if you cannot directly overcome a powerful authority, you can decide to ignore it, or resist it with guile and cunning. At the same time she is giving us an example of how a writer can choose to work, insisting on the validity of her own perceptions and, crucially, mixing one kind of text with another. Sido's saucy rhetoric sets her up as Colette's muse. Her voice resounds through the house of imagination; she instructs, scolds, soothes, sings.

So far so tender and affectionate. However, Sido is not only the straightforwardly admirable heroine of fairy tales and myths, not only the smiling country goddess who presides over harvests and bears in apples and flowers and corn, not only the fairy godmother who rescues starving children and stray animals. She can frown. She can even seem to curse.

A discordant tone marks Colette's account of Sido's attitude to her older daughter, Juliette, a child of Sido's first marriage, who is presented as unsociable, difficult, and Different in a negative way. Juliette has a 'strange head, of attractive ugliness, with high cheekbones' and 'a sarcastic mouth … thick eyebrows', a low forehead and black 'Mongol' eyes (*LMC* 74; *MMHS* 78). Michèle Sarde sees these eyes as possibly the result of her alcoholic heritage. Sido's first husband was addicted to drink and died as a result of it. In addition to her distinctive face, Juliette has 'abnormally long', over-exuberant dark hair, reaching to her feet once loosed and veiling her completely.

In the nineteenth century into which Colette was born, women's long hair had what Nicole Ward Jouve calls 'a loaded history'. She cites Baudelaire's 'La Chevelure', 'followed by countless others ... Symbolist and "Decadent" representations of women's hair' that linked it to perverse sexuality and entrapment (NWJ 93). Long-haired women are mermaids, beautiful but monstrous. Their hair becomes a net for capturing men, entangling them, pulling them down to death by drowning. Baudelaire's muse and lover, Jeanne Duval, had long, thick black hair. In his poem it springs alive in a series of metaphors invoking desire that coil just like the hair itself: a magnificent fleece, a scented sea, an exotic foreign island. Jeanne is the quintessential Other: female and black.

Sido speaks of Juliette's hair as 'an incurable evil'. She claims it as her duty to brush and comb it, complaining of her task. Colette writes: 'I would see my mother, worn out, come down the stairs from the first floor, throwing down the paraphernalia of brushes and combs: "I'm done for...I've just been combing Juliette's hair"' (LMC 74; MMHS 78). Snakes appear in the biblical myth of Eden as malevolent, as in Greek myths do Medusas with snaky locks, and Juliette's hair gets done up into heavy plaits 'shiny as water-snakes', into 'a sort of ridiculous crown' in front, and 'another cake' on the nape of her neck (LMC 74; MMHS 79).

In another layer of reference in this tale of Juliette, Sido takes on the persona of Rapunzel's mother. One way to keep your daughter chained to you at home is to weigh her down with her own hair and not allow her to cut it. Mother and daughter become tied together inextricably. Juliette's hair, enclosing her completely, becomes the imprisoning tower itself.

Colette's equally long 'golden' hair, on the other hand, is Sido's delight and pride, the gold balanced against the black and found superior. Sido refers to it as her own possession, her own treasure. Judith Thurman writes about Sido's lack of boundaries, her overidentification with her favourite daughter: 'She was as proprietary of her children's bodies as she was "oversolicitous" about their feelings. Her daughter's hair, for example, was her "masterpiece", and she complained when Colette—a woman of thirty—cut it without permission' (SF 30).

Blackness and darkness are not neutral adjectives in the story of Juliette. They have a particular meaning and history in western culture, which first of all referred pejoratively to the slaves transported from Africa as non-Christians, as opposed to their Christian owners, and then, once slaves started being converted to Christianity, started to use black and white as markers of difference constructed by power. Sido, Colette's biographers tell us, has African heritage. Margaret Crosland, in her 1954 biography of Colette, sees this as negative and unpleasant. She spells it out in her first chapter: Sido's father 'was a quarteroon, with purple fingernails, and was known as "the Gorilla" because of his thick, terrifying negro mouth. His daughter Sidonie never forgave him for passing it on to her.'[4] I see, looking at my copy of Crosland's text, which I bought second hand and read in the early 1980s, that I marked these lines and next to them wrote 'What!?!'. Crosland gives no reference for this passage, so it is impossible to check her source. (The rest of her book, written while Colette was still alive, addresses itself to the Great Writer and reads like a fan letter, interesting only as an example of how biography can become hagiography. Juliette is hardly mentioned.)

Perhaps Crosland is referring to the more nuanced passage in the chapter in *La Maison de Claudine* entitled 'La "Fille de mon Père"' ('My "Father's Daughter"'), which I have mentioned above. This certainly contains a jarring racist trope, Sido's (and Colette's) acceptance of Henry Landoy's acquaintances giving him a racist nickname, but does not show Sido labelling his mouth 'terrifying' and 'negro', as Crosland does. It is Colette who mentions 'the negro mouth'. Describing her father's appearance, Sido employs the adjective *vilain*, an adjective with various meanings: unpleasant, or bad looking/ugly, or nasty, as in a nasty wound. Sido is reminiscencing to the child Colette.

> 'Ah! That Gorilla. You can see how ugly he was, Minet-Chéri. And yet so many women dangled after him'. She pointed with her thimble at the daguerreotype hanging on the wall, the same daguerreotype that I now keep in a drawer, and which reveals, under its silvery tarnish, the head and shoulders of a coloured man—a quadroon, I think—with a high white cravat, pale, scornful eyes, a long nose above the negro mouth that had earned him his nickname.... 'Ugly, but well-made ... And attractive too, I repeat, despite his purple fingernails. I resent him only for giving me his ugly mouth'. She had a wide mouth, it is true, but good-tempered and red. (*LMC* 62; *MMHS* 69)

When I look at photographs of Sido, I think her wide mouth gives her a distinctive charm, helps form the beauty of her face. Colette, by contrast, has a simpering, skimpy, sharp bow emphasized by her way with a lipstick. Fast forward to our own times, when thin mouths are out of fashion and certain aspects of African beauty are appropriated and commodified by westerners through cosmetic surgery and fake tans.

In the vignettes featuring Juliette in *La Maison de Claudine*, Colette does seem to me to compose a portrait of Juliette that makes her 'darkness' a negative not a neutral term. The political marker becomes also a psychological one, indicating mystery, unknowability, possible mental illness, the threat of violence. Michèle Sarde, giving no evidence for her view, remarks 'the girl was completely schizoid, and would encounter one of her brothers in the house with surprise' (CFF 50).

We are in fairy-tale land again, with its deployment of simplistic opposites, the Good Sister shadowed by the Bad Sister. Colette is constantly acknowledged, addressed, seen, understood by Sido, whereas Juliette seems written off. How much of this is Sido's responsibility, that she did actually ignore and neglect her older daughter, and how much is this simply Colette's version?

Juliette was Sido's daughter by her first husband, Claude Jules Robineau-Duclos. Sido was handed over to him by her brothers, despite his being what Francis and Gontier call 'difficult to marry off' (FG 27). He was thought to inherit the psychological instability that saw his mother and uncle interned in asylums. I speculate that perhaps Sido made Juliette into a reminder of her unhappy marriage to that difficult man. Perhaps she scapegoated her, projected onto her certain feelings of rage and resentment that she could not tolerate inside herself. Francis and Gontier also point out that Sido's second husband, Jules Colette, was a neglectful stepfather who took little notice or care of Juliette.

If long-haired Juliette can be read as Rapunzel, she can be seen as struggling to become the heroine of her own story. She dreams up acts of resistance. If she can hide herself under her cascading hair, she can also retreat into books. Colette portrays herself as an avid reader, but a well-balanced one, always willing to stop reading and enjoy other things, such as escaping into the countryside. She portrays her sister, by contrast, as taking a love of books to excessive lengths. Reading becomes less a way of delighting in language and imagination than a form of addiction:

> Always pale and absorbed, she read in a grim kind of way ... She read, while mechanically winding one of her serpents of hair around her wrist, and sometimes, without seeing me, let her glance wander towards me, that glance of an obsessive that is ageless and sexless, full of obscure defiance and impenetrable irony. (LMC 75; MMHS 79)

Colette does not attempt to explore why her sister feels the need to become an obsessive reader, whether it is to do with a need to escape her life and her family, or to imagine various different selves for herself through imaginative identifications with the protagonists of novels, or to imagine different lives and fates other than the conventional future of marriage and childbearing. She simply describes how Juliette retires into non-stop reading. The implication is that Colette's love of books is healthy and sane whereas Juliette's is pathological. When Colette breaks into Juliette's reverie and asks her what she is reading, 'Juliette's reply was long, long in coming, as though leagues of space and of silence separated us' (LMC 76; MMHS 79). She mentions novels such as *The Charterhouse of Parma*, *The Vicar of Wakefield*, *Les Misérables*. She also devours poetry, magazines, and romances.

The fairy-tale mood intensifies. Colette's account suggests that Juliette has been bewitched by books, snatched away by them as though they are the kidnapping fairies of old tales. She lives in a dreamworld, as though she has fallen asleep, like the Sleeping Beauty: 'my long-haired sister no longer spoke, hardly ate, jerked with surprise if she met us about the house, came to with a start if someone rang the bell' (*LMC* 77; *MMHS* 80). Juliette reads in bed at night, too, by lamplight, by candlelight, by the glimmer of a nightlight, by the light of matches, by moonlight: 'after the moonlight, my long-haired sister, worn out by novel-induced insomnia, caught a fever, and this fever persisted, despite compresses and doses of purgatives' (*LMC* 77; *MMHS* 81). Perhaps on one level this illness offers Juliette another form of escape from whatever is troubling her, an escape towards a fantasy of freedom. She babbles, in her delirium, of necessarily secret meetings with imaginary suitors: '"no, we shan't meet anyone … In any case, I don't know anyone in these parts. I know no-one here." My sister stopped speaking, moaned in a bitter and intolerant way, turned to the wall and continued to moan in a very low voice, as though from far away' (*LMC* 78; *MMHS* 82).

For Sido, Juliette has become 'a stranger, who in her delirium summons only other strangers'. For me, Juliette is speaking her truth: she is indeed a stranger in the household. The people who should love her do not understand her. They treat her like one of the changelings invoked in Irish fairy stories. She has been bewitched, and she may bewitch them in turn. They seem afraid of her, tiptoeing around her, keeping their distance.

Juliette's obsession reminds me of the similar one of Flaubert's Emma Bovary. His protagonist's tragedy has a source in her overidentification with the heroines in the romances to which she is addicted and her desire to make her banal life match up to their glamorous goings-on. Like Madame Bovary, Juliette makes a sudden and unfortunate marriage, bears a child, and comes to a self-inflicted bad end. Having made a suicide attempt early in her marriage, she makes another later on and does succeed in killing herself. Her doctor husband, avaricious and litigious, seems to have exacerbated her problems. What are the reasons for Juliette's choice of him as husband? To spite her family? To follow a first romantic desire? To clutch at any available suitor? They are certainly not spelled out in *La Maison de Claudine*. We are simply given a sense of the villagers' malicious pleasure that an ageing spinster of nearly 30 has secured a husband at last.

Romances, some feminists argue,[5] rehearsed urgent questions for women, particularly in times when divorce was difficult, around the selection of a husband. How do I know if he is any good/can be trusted/ is secretly misogynistic/prone to violence? According to this view, women's reading of romances, far from being frivolous and valueless, embodies a sort of imaginative research, even if the romances return reassuringly (damningly?) in the end to the status quo of marital bliss. Living happily ever after becomes a commandment. Juliette does not manage it.

She lives out one classic aspect of romances: the heroine is isolated, with no female friends to give her support; she fights her battles alone. Juliette's break with her family, occasioned by bitter, unresolved wrangling over her dowry and settlements (problems dating back to her parents' wedding contract), sees Juliette physically exiled, living close to her parents and siblings, on the other side of their garden wall, yet completely removed in terms of contact and affection.

The fairy tale develops towards a domestically based horror story. If daughters, on one level, mirror their mothers, Colette's manipulation of the looking glass splits the image of the daughter in two. Juliette seems to stand for the negative side of Sido, and Colette for the positive. Juliette becomes (like her aunt Irma) the kind of unfortunate not spoken of in a bourgeois family, since she disturbs its complacent view of its own solidity and happiness; a ghost haunting the shadowy margins of the narrative. She has been repressed by the familial will; forgotten about. Colette's expressed distance towards her sister may have to do with tact and compassion on her part, but nonetheless chills me. Juliette seems to have been made into the outsider.

Perhaps I feel that partly because I remember how I exiled myself from my own family in my twenties, or felt exiled from it, in a tangle of conflicted feelings. I longed to flee and find freedom, and also to return and belong. Becoming involved in feminism, in left-wing politics, experimenting with sex, not getting married, living in a series of communal households rather than aspiring to owning property, scraping a freelance living, I knew my parents vehemently disapproved of me. At that time, I heard their outrage, not their concern. I felt that I was necessarily an outcast who could not possibly be received at home again. At least my angry confusion let me leave home, pushed me to write books, permitted me to spend hours every day reading just like Juliette. Now I can see that writing was my bid for freedom, my struggle for it. Writing was also, in the end, my way of returning to my mother, to building a better relationship with her. Finally, we apologized to each other; affirmed our love for each other. Now I recognize how I want to reunite Colette and Juliette, as I wanted to reunite inside myself what they represented: the split-apart good daughter and bad daughter.

This splitting of Sido's daughters into the loved one and the rejected/rejecting one means that Colette's loving image of Sido survives intact. Yet, to see Sido as so good, you have to ignore her difficulties with Juliette, what seems at the very least her ambivalence towards her. On my first reading of *La Maison de Claudine* I envied Colette having such an apparently perfect mother, not least one who talked to her, accepted her, encouraged her. On this later reading, filtering those first impressions through the versions of family life given by Colette's biographers, I do start to wonder.

Judith Thurman, as I mentioned above, sees Sido as flawed rather than perfect, as ignoring certain boundaries that should exist between a mother and her children, regarding their bodies as hers, as extensions of herself. In the vignette 'Maternity', Colette sketches a positive version of this—how fictional it is of course impossible to say. Once Juliette is pregnant, Sido identifies with her, developing certain physical symptoms:

> the rumour reached us, one day, that she was going to have a baby. But I hardly thought about her anymore and I took no notice of the fact that at precisely this time my mother began to suffer from nervous fits of dizziness, upset stomach, and palpitations …She began to express her energies in a rather disturbed way. One day she put salt rather than sugar in the strawberry tart, and met my father's reproaches with a closed, ironic look that amazed me. (*LMC* 80; *MMHS* 82)

Once Juliette is actually in labour, Sido enters her garden, bordering her daughter's, and shares in her daughter's pain, acting out a form of maternal magic:

> Then I saw my mother determinedly grip her own haunches, and twist round on herself, and pound the ground with her feet, and she began helping and taking upon herself, with low groans and the rocking of her tormented body and the clutching of her unwanted arms, with all her suffering and maternal force, the suffering and force of the ungrateful daughter who, so far from her, was giving birth. (*LMC* 83; *MMHS* 85)

The 'ungrateful daughter' has escaped into what seems an unhappy marriage. Sido's own first marriage is certainly not shown as happy. In the chapter of *La Maison de Claudine* entitled 'Le Sauvage' ('The Wild Man'), concerning Sido's first husband, Colette tells us Robineau-Duclos was given his nickname on account of his liking to ride out hunting alone, all day long, without even a dog as a companion. She recounts the story of Sido's marriage as a version of Beauty and the Beast mixed with hints of Bluebeard. In this version, the two protagonists meet by chance, in true romantic style, when blonde, ringleted Sido has been visiting her old nurse in northern France and the Wild Man, who has lands nearby, rides past. Sido, taking note of his 'black beard, strawberry roan horse, distinguished vampire's pallor' (*LMC* 11; *MMHS* 28), attracts him by looking at him without lowering her eyes or smiling. She is more of a challenge than the women servants he feels entitled to seduce (fuck) then discard. She is frightened and silenced by his proposal of marriage: 'but a young girl with neither fortune nor employment, financially dependent on her brothers, has nothing to do but shut up, take her chance and thank God' (*LMC* 12; *MMHS* 29).

He whisks her away from her family and friends, their bohemian world of painters, musicians, and poets. Colette employs the verb *enlever à*, which in some contexts refers to kidnapping and abduction, and in this one hints at a snatching that underlines the fairy-tale element of the story. The vignette/chapter entitled 'Le Sauvage' occupies only four pages, and inside it the account of Sido's first marriage nestles like a tiny novel. Perhaps it is all the more powerful for being so tiny, composed of just a few dramatic details: it expands in our imaginations, like those Japanese screws of paper we had in childhood, that you plunged into a glass of water and watched bloom into many-petalled flowers.

The Wild Man lives in a mansion, gone to mouldering rack and ruin, in the depths of a forested landscape. In fairy tales, forests are classically sites of adventure, strange encounters with wild beasts and witches, danger and transformation. Sido's marriage is itself a forest, all-encompassing and forbidding, peopled with creatures who may be untrustworthy or turn violent. She is trapped in it. Having been handed over, removed from her warm, cheerful Belgian home lively with conversation and music, she tries to settle in

> the country mansion cut off in the harsh winters by the forests surrounding it … The icy bedrooms spoke neither of love nor of restful sleep. Silverware … cut glass and wine abounded. Shadowy old women sat spinning by candlelight in the kitchen at evening, stripping and winding the flax grown on the estate, making linen, heavy, hard-wearing, and cold, for bedroom and household use. The harsh prattle of bad-tempered cooks rose and fell, depending on whether the master left or approached the house; bearded old fairies cast ill-wishing glances at the young bride, and some good-looking young washerwoman abandoned by the master sobbed noisily, leaning against the well, whenever the Wild Man was out hunting … In her home Sido encountered only servants, tongue-tied farmers, and gamekeepers sticky with wine and the blood of hares, who left a smell of wolves behind them. To them the Wild Man spoke infrequently, arrogantly. The descendant of a once-noble family, he retained his forebears' disdain, courtesy, brutality, taste for low company. (LMC 12; MMHS 30)

Sido, relishing wit, wordplay, and conversation, is lonely. The taciturn new husband 'smiled at her in between two outings, then left again'. Did he stay silent at night too in their 'icy' bedroom? Colette does not tell us, as presumably Sido would not have told her, but she makes me imagine a speechless lovemaking, better simply called sex acts, a lack of playfulness and sensuality. Gallant Sido makes the best of things and works her feminine magic: 'she filled the great house with flowers, had the dark kitchen whitewashed, supervised the preparation of Flemish dishes, stirred mixtures for fruit cakes, and hoped to become pregnant.' Meanwhile, her dour mate has 'returned to his vines, his swampy forests'. To Sido's company he prefers 'lingering in inns at crossroads, where around one tall candle everything is dark: the rafters, the smoke-blackened walls, the rye bread and the wine in metal goblets' (*LMC* 13; *MMHS* 30).

In a traditional legend such as 'Patient Griselda', the grumpy, taciturn husband would be transformed by his wife's unselfishness and courage, learn to love and cherish her. In this one, the Wild Man, seeing traces of tears on Sido's face and realizing she's missing something, brings her two presents: a marble pestle and mortar and a cashmere shawl. (You try to pound your wife into submission and then you bandage her consolingly in a shawl.) Colette ends the story there, with the husband dumbly presenting his gifts and Sido describing, years later, to her daughter, how she saw her husband, on that occasion, as like a dog returning from foraging with a tiny slipper in its jaws. The reader enjoys a shudder, wondering whether the slipper belonged to some poor child eaten by wolves, or perhaps to one of the Cinderellas who does not make it to the ball but gets waylaid by a bloodthirsty ogre who snatches her up and makes off with her.

If Sido was handed over to a neglectful, drunkard husband, if Juliette was handed over to a greedy, difficult one, Colette domesticates the image of kidnap and rapture by giving herself a starring role in her own version of such a story. Now the mother masquerades as the ogre. Once Juliette has married and left home, Colette moves into her sister's bedroom on an upper floor, distant from her mother's. Previously she has slept in a 'den', connecting with her mother's room, over the carriage entrance. Sido, listening to village rumours of burglars, nervous of villainous male intruders, mentions remembering that, 'at Ghent, when I was young, one of our friends who was only sixteen was abducted … There could be no question of returning her to her family … In the end they got married. There was no other way out' (LMC 28; MMHS 42) (Francis and Gontier suggest that this is a cryptic reference to the fate of Sido's half-sister Irma). Colette, intrigued by the tale, suddenly notices an engraving hanging in a dark passage, showing a young girl being manhandled by her swain into a carriage. The title of the image is *The Abduction*. Then one night when the yard doors are rattling and gusts of wind sweep in under the loose-fitting slates just above Colette's head, Sido whirls into the little girl's bedroom, snatches her up, and carries her down to her former room. Colette records her delight in being helpless, in thrall, to the powerful maternal Other. The comedy of the piece revolves around the child waking next morning in now unfamiliar surroundings and crying out: mother, come quickly! I've been abducted!

Germaine Greer once speculated that the kiss at the end of traditional romances stood for the orgasm unmentionable in that coy context. Perhaps the bodice-ripping hero of the romance can, on one level, stand for the all-powerful abductor–mother, and vice versa. Colette hints at the link:

> Did I wake, in any case? I doubt it. Only a dream, with a single flap of its wing, could snatch a little girl out of her childhood and set

her down, neither surprised nor rebellious, in the midst of a hypocritical and adventurous adolescence. Only a dream can make a
child of tender age blossom into the ungrateful creature she will be
tomorrow, the double-dealing accomplice of a passer-by. (*LMC* 29;
MMHS 43)

Heroines in the bodice-ripper style of romances are at first distressed by being overpowered and helpless, before finally learning
to enjoy settling into their proper feminine place. Colette's account
of fantasy and imagination is many-layered and subtle, invoking
childhood sexuality alongside the metamorphosis of the child
into the young woman, the dream itself being the abductor.

How much is a victim–heroine straightforwardly at the mercy
of her captor and how much is she complicit in complicated ways?
Judith Thurman, discussing Colette's abject role vis-à-vis her first
two husbands, links her submissiveness to masochism and links
this in turn to infantile experience and the adult's attempts to
master it (*SF, passim*). I do see that taking up the role of masochist
can permit the re-enactment of those longings to be safely held,
controlled, dandled, snatched up, borne off, even as it allows the
pain experienced in helpless childhood to be rechoreographed
by the knowing adult. Physical pain can stand in for emotional
pain. The masochist collaborates with the sadist, can even be said
to be in control. She does not have to accept her own aggression
and rage, since the sadist carries it for her. On the other hand,
this psychoanalytical approach, while compelling, omits cultural
factors. I would agree with the feminists who consider that, in
an alienated and male-dominated world, women are unfree and
make alienated choices.

I would also want to listen, however, to Marion Milner, who,
discussing ego-surrender in *A Life of One's Own*,[6] suggests that it

can be liberating. Wholeheartedly, in situations of difficulty and blockedness, admitting one's incapacity to act, can paradoxically allow the finding of solutions. Milner seems also to be saying that occasional ego-surrender, letting go of being in control, can fulfil deep psychological needs for balance and release. If you do not know how to do it, then discipline can help you get there, find that bliss. Religious prayer practices, carefully taught, offer one route, for example. S-M, carefully choreographed, perhaps offers another. Experiments in trust and dependence? Suddenly I am reminded of the poet Rilke saying (I do not remember where) something to the effect that when seeking inspiration in writing you have to jump off the cliff and then the angel arrives and bears you up on his wings. Perhaps to meet the angel you have first to meet your own fear. Perhaps the fear turns into the angel. At any rate, however I decide to regard the possibility that a sadist is a parent in disguise, thinking about masochism's complexities helps me understand Colette's interest in so-called perversion, her recognition of the bondage of conventional gender roles, the liberating shifts in power that sex games may entail, layers of identity whisked on and off like strippers' veils.

Rereading the vignette 'The Abduction' I relish Colette's sub-tlety about girls' complicated desires and their wishes to explore them through fantasy. I also come up against certain material facts. Colette's amused account of her child self being whirled away by Sido makes it clear that the family lives in a large house, not a peasant cottage. I did not see this when I first read *La Maison de Claudine*. Remembering it, I retained primarily images of the inviting outdoors described, a sense of the book's entrancing celebration of the natural world beyond the family home and the child Colette's freedom to explore it, to come home muddy and wet, pockets full of foraged treasures. Revelling in this account of liberty, I saw only the forests and fields the child roamed through, not the bourgeois village house to which she returned. I did not notice the class position of Colette's family. I assumed that Colette, writing with such detailed, intimate knowledge of country life, country lore, came from a simple, peasant background. How did I manage to ignore her mentions of the cook, the horse and trap, the house with its imposing street façade? I must have read selectively, concentrating on the writing about escapes to the woods and streams, the solitary explorations and walks. They were certainly what I longed for. Colette was so much freer than I was when I stayed with my bourgeois French grandparents in the tight little world of their Norman village; therefore, I reasoned childishly, she came from a different class, one that allowed liberty to its children.

My French grandparents lived in an 1890s redbrick cottage on the edge of the village, in easy walking distance of church and shops, and about a kilometre from the farms, going the other way. The smallness of their house, compared with the large white manor house opposite set in spacious grounds, hid the fact that my grandparents were firmly middle class. Before the war they had lived in a house in Le Havre, close to the docks, where Grandpère was head engineer. Grandmère had been his secretary. Once war broke out, Grandpère removed the family to their country cottage, where they went on living after the docks were bombed to bits and their house there destroyed. They stayed on in the village when the war finally ended. They had a car, and for some years, before the war, employed a live-in maid. Grandpère had converted the attic into tiny bedrooms. The maid's had a single bed, a narrow cupboard built into the eave, a washbasin, a small window in the sloping roof. It later became my elder sister's bedroom. Mine, shared with my twin sister, doubled as the linen room, where on wet days sheets could be hung to dry. Even though the cottage was on the edge of the countryside, fields and woods just down the road, we children did not roam about. We would not have dared do that. My grandparents maintained their social distance from the farms, the farming people. On our decorous family walks, we kept, boringly, to the road. When I went back, many years later, with Jim, my husband, he consulted maps and worked out an eight-kilometre route through woods and deep valleys to the sea at Etretat, all on footpaths, and I was amazed and delighted.

Rereading *La Maison de Claudine* I now see that the child Colette was the one who happily mixed with peasants, not the adult Sido. She ticked off her little daughter for relishing what she deemed the vulgarity of 'servants' weddings' and the ungenteel rituals enjoyed by shopkeepers' children. If the mother is the presiding goddess in a country paradise, she is also the bearer of the urban-dictated bourgeois rulebook. Sido bent the rules to suit herself as much as she could, but nonetheless she had to live inside them.

One obvious example of such a rule, perhaps more of an accepted custom, was the requirement for adult children to leave home on marriage. Sido did not want to part with her children and resisted this. In 'The Abduction' she equates Juliette's marriage with her 'going off with a gentleman she hardly knows'. Colette treats this as comedy; her critics see it as Sido's possessiveness. At any rate, Juliette fell riskily in love. In English we say: don't get carried away! Earlier I mentioned that Colette described Sido's first marriage as her being snatched away, carried away, from her family. Carried off.

Carried across? That is the meaning of translation, which comes from the Latin. To be translated is to be carried across. Translating Colette's work into English, I am carried away from my French mother, at the same time carrying her image with me; I am carrying my thoughts back to her by reading her language, and this recalls her voice.

I first read *La Maison de Claudine* in English. Reading it now in French, swimming in the French language, I feel my French self, my French daughterliness, revive inside me, expand me; a feeling of intense pleasure. My Frenchness does feel buried sometimes, as though I cannot live it out while I am in England, except for being aware of a dim sense of not really belonging. Did my mother feel that, marrying an Englishman and settling in England? She tried her best to become English. I made a fictionalized portrait of her doing that, and also periodically resisting it, in my novel *Cut Out* (2021). I wrote about autobiography and translation in my short story 'Une Glossaire' ('A Glossary') (1993). Mum enjoyed pointing out that *glossaire* is masculine. Trust me to have made it feminine. I wrote about translation and identity, translation as identity, in *Daughters of the House* (1992), imagining the English language metamorphosing into the French one in mid-Channel, far beneath the surface of the sea; hybrid; a sort of monster. Travelling by Eurostar across to France, between languages, feeling one change into the other inside me, I feel fluid, changeable, belonging at that point of metamorphosis, at home deep down under the water. Departing and returning.

When I am in France, speaking French more or less fluently, I am nonetheless seen by my neighbours as a foreigner, though a well-meaning one ('at least you're not a Parisian'). Writing this book helps me reconnect my split-apart French and English selves, because I am translating from French into English.

However, in attempting to translate the passages I want to quote, I have had to grapple with a beginner's difficulties. I have never translated a literary text before. Colette's language and style, employing compression, a mixture of archaic and contemporary vocabulary, and idiosyncratic grammar, are not easy to render into English. Raymond Mortimer, in his introduction to the translation of *Chéri* by Roger Senhouse, compared Colette's imagination to that of Picasso and asserted:

> She can foreshorten the French language as boldly as Mallarmé; she has it trained to obey her caprices like a pony in a circus. All of which is a perpetual feast to the reader, a chronic headache to the translator ... The difficulty of translating her is more nearly desperate than anyone knows who has not tried his hand at it.[7]

To discuss *La Maison de Claudine*, matching the French original against English versions of it, I have been consulting the translation made for Secker and Warburg in 1953 by Una Troubridge and Enid McLeod. Even as a beginner translator, I am surprised by how much I disagree with certain of their versions. For example, in their descriptions of the Wild Man, they give us his 'youthful' black beard, when youthful does not occur in the original, just 'barbe noire'. (Impossible not to think of Barbe Bleue/Bluebeard.) Also, when the French distinctly has 'sa paleur de vampire distingué', this is rendered as romantic pallor. The vampire is erased. Such unnecessary alterations weaken the hints of fairy tale and horror.

Rereading *La Maison de Claudine* for the second time this week, I now find it invokes yet another distinctive literary form, one that embraces the others discussed above. It can be read as a

Bildungsroman, a novel about becoming. It creates a picture of a writer formed by maternal inspiration: Sido's unconventional versions of dominant teachings, Sido's language, Sido's stories, Sido's opinions on her daughter's reading. Colette paints a picture of a mother who knew how to take and hold her listener's attention with her distinctive turns of phrase, her knowledge of how to control and compress narrative, how to twist an ending into shape. Colette learned storytelling long before she met Willy and was obliged by him to start writing the Claudine books. She often insisted, perhaps disingenuously, that she had had no intention of becoming a writer, but she had the knowledge of how to begin stored inside her, harvested from her childhood, from her closeness to Sido.

Halt. Am I oversimplifying? It seems so. It seems that in fact Colette had two women mothering her into becoming a writer. Francis and Gontier suggest that the second source of inspiration was Colette's wetnurse, Emilie Fleurie, who looked after her for four years (and inspired the figure of the nanny, Mélie, in the Claudine books). Émilie had her own daughter, and breastfed both children. Sido stuck up for Émilie, the single mother, in those days an object of scandal. Later, when Colette was 8, Émilie returned to the household and became the family cook. She delighted her protégée with her exhaustive knowledge of folklore and folk tales: 'she increased Gabri's delight "with a precious terror" by telling her tales of the wolves that in very cold winters could still be seen prowling around the farms' (FG 41).

Émilie was Colette's link to the local peasant world, its skills, cuisine, culture, festivals, paganism, legends. Sido, for all her gardening and cookery lore, disdained village arts and pleasures, remaining conscious of her formation in a family of intellectuals and writers. Colette had the good fortune to be nourished by two streams of language, two streams of storytelling. Early on, she left the provinces for Paris, but she retained certain provincial attitudes, as her biographers have pointed out. She gives to Léa in *Chéri* her own knowledge of careful housewifery and thrifty housekeeping. She could swerve between being a worldly, urbane, Parisian wordspinner and the epitome of the village soothsayer quoting ancient recipes, charms, and spells. Just as she learned traditional lewd songs from Émilie, so she could pick out a tune in front of a famous modernist musician. Nicole Ward Jouve tells us 'Colette was a good pianist ... She gloried in having been able to reproduce on the piano, and sing, a tune which she had just heard with Debussy, and which Debussy could not recollect. He looked at M. Willy's country-wife like never before, and said gently, "Welcome ..."' (NWJ 28).

Rereading *La Maison de Claudine*, admiring its sophisticated and subtle deployment of tropes from fairy tales, romances, oral anecdotes, horror, I want to explore why I asserted above that I think those references crucial. Why did Colette employ them? In what way do they form and embellish her story of her becoming?

The fragmented form of this collection of vignettes does give an effect of spontaneity, of sketches dashed off, of realism, particularly when, as above, I compare them to photographs, particularly of family gatherings, apparently immediate rather than composed. Yet, thinking about this, I see that the pictures of Colette and her family, reproduced in the biographies, are carefully posed, with hierarchies observed. *La Maison de Claudine* may evoke the seeming informality of the family album, but the fairy tale and mythical elements suggest that something else may be going on at the same time. Affectionate memoir may be mixed with fantasy. Nowadays we commonsensically accept that memory and memoir are unreliable, that an apparently artless account is a carefully constructed story, that a writer may consciously or unconsciously shape her autobiographical material to provide her desired effect. Therefore, I shall ask: what was Colette's?

I said above that Sido is presented as a goddess. I mean specifically Demeter, the queen of harvests, in charge of the fruitfulness and abundance of the earth. In the Greek myth, when her daughter, Persephone, is snatched away from her and carried down to the underworld, Demeter follows and rescues her. We have seen how Sido was intent on doing that for Colette, in the latter's playful account of being snatched up in the middle of the night. However, Sido could not manage it for her daughter Juliette.

In the myth, Demeter has to learn to let her daughter go, in order to welcome her back. Together they invent a dance, a ritual, of letting go and drawing back, of leaving and returning, so that winter may regularly, annually, relinquish its clutches on the cold, barren earth and usher in the warm, fertile spring. Judith Thurman points out on and off, throughout her biography, that, even with her favoured daughter, Colette, Sido did not quite achieve this harmonious rhythm. Colette, once having left home, rarely returned. She did not attend her mother's funeral. She composed a portrait of a mother attuned to nature, cherishing and respecting living beings, a personage lively and benevolent and vigorous to the end, but she chose, as an adult, not to spend much time with her. How much is too much time? Is Colette, in this resolutely loving portrait of Sido, idealizing her, thereby hiding a certain ambivalence? A certain complexity of feeling? Love and hate may be normal in a daughter, in that as much as you love your mother you may need also to 'hate' her in order to leave her and grow up, and then feel able to get close to her again, but it may be possible to feel too much love, and so never leave, or too much hate, and so feel unable to return. Colette, once having left, seems to have needed to maintain a certain distance. Too much? How much is too much distance? Did Colette ever even for just one moment hate Sido? It is impossible to know. Sido is presented as ideal and perfect, as impossible to hate. That is that. It is the biographers such as Thurman and the critics such as Brunet who unpick the golden threads of the tapestry.

The fairy-tale and mythical elements in *La Maison de Claudine* do not only serve, if unsteadily, the function of idealization. They reveal its purpose. They both point something out and at the same time veil it, almost hide it completely.

Let me look again at Colette's vivid picture of Sido's first marriage. I am entranced by that chapter's Gothic feel, its chiaroscuro colouring, its picture of the brave young wife working in the dark, cavernous kitchen, I am reminded of Cocteau's black-and-white film *La Belle et La Bête*. Colette makes it all sound quite appealing. However, when I read Francis and Gontier, I am distressed by what they spell out about Robineau, twenty years Sido's senior. He was not only severely alcoholic but when drunk frequently became physically violent. Certainly, at that time it was accepted, in a commonsensical way, that men were matter of factly capable of domestic violence, to be subsequently excused for it, but Robineau sounds like a particularly gross monster. Francis and Gontier make me see that Robineau not only inflicted suffering on others but suffered himself: 'this was a traumatized being who was afraid of shadows and could not bear being left alone at night' (FG 28).

Under the adult monster's skin hides the child. The fear of being left alone may have connected to a fear of dependence matched by a fear of abandonment, such as a neglected child may feel. The child's unbearable anger, which threatens to overwhelm him, may be projected into the shadows that threaten in their turn. Later, women may bear the brunt of the need for revenge and punishment. Francis and Gontier recount that Robineau grew up 'like a wild beast'. He was frightening to look at, since he had two rows of teeth, having retained his early, milk ones. When he was 16, an itinerant barber, armed with a pair of pincers and a bottle of eau-de-vie, wrenched out the surplus teeth. This trauma was preceded by another. The year before, Robineau's mother had been shut up in an asylum. No one is recorded as helping the youth cope. He grew up troubled by rages he could not control. He lived with Marie Miton, the young servant who was his *concubine* (a legal term in France for an unmarried female lover–companion), and regularly beat her, to such an extent that she felt driven to send her baby away to her sister for safety. He went on cohabiting with Marie after his marriage to Sido; Marie was the one person who could calm his delirious rages. He had hallucinations of attackers. He threatened to murder servants who displeased him. Colette does not mention these episodes.

Whether I like it or not, her biographers' pictures of Sido's first marriage clash with Colette's and afford it a much grimmer aspect. She gives us a highly coloured romance. They put down bleak facts. Robineau did not fall in love with Sido at first sight as she skipped along in the forest, as Colette's sanitized story suggests. Sido was not a poor maiden whom he romantically endowed with his hand, but an heiress, albeit encumbered by debts, who was handed over like an object by her brothers. The deal was seen by Jules's family as a way of settling him down and quashing any future financial claims Marie Miton might make on behalf of her son (she was hastily married off, with a settlement, to a much younger man), and by Sido's relatives as a way for her to continue in her luxury-loving lifestyle. All dispiritingly materialistic and unromantic.

In the quick sketches of Juliette, the fairy-tale aspect of her story represses harsh and painful facts. Casting Juliette as the Rapunzel who gets away by faulty means from her anxious mother, as the 'bad' Rapunzel who is seduced by the wrong prince climbing up her plaits, Colette pushes a family difficulty, a family injustice, to one remove and keeps it there. She tells us how, as a child, she developed a way of stubbornly resisting those texts that displeased her: to Perrault's versions of fairy tales she preferred the graphic images of Gustave Doré and Walter Crane. 'Not one word of his crossed the threshold I was barring to him. Where do they go, later, this enormous willed ignorance, this tranquil force employed for banning, for removing oneself?' (LMC 36; MMHS 48). Perhaps they can be employed in refusing to read between the lines of family stories.

Juliette functions like an ink blot on the margin of the golden page of Colette's prose. She can be regretted and then ignored. Pushed to one side, she goes on signalling to me. I speculate (with no proof) that Juliette is made to stand for any pain and suffering felt by Colette and subsequently omitted from her account of her 'happy childhood'. However, she is also herself, a real person with a problematic life and a tragic death.

Juliette having been erased, Colette can achieve her object of presenting herself as Sido's favourite daughter. Sido can be idealized precisely because she has chosen to love Colette more than her half-sister. All the recounted scoldings and upbraidings and criticisms function to underline Sido's attention focussed solely on Colette, endlessly attentive to her, concerned with her. Sido appears to bother far more with her child than with the child's 'poor father'. The husband may be devoted, may catch his wife's hand and kiss it as she passes, may long for her return when she has gone off on a round of village visits, but he is pushed aside as slightly ridiculous in his neediness; it is the little daughter who matters more.

Colette goes further, presenting herself also as Sido's favourite child *tout court*. She is the golden apple of Sido's golden eye. They exchange unbroken gazes. They exist with and for only each other. Sido's adoring nicknames for Colette (treasure, beauty, jewel set in gold) contrast with how she names her brothers: *les sauvages*. (Why did Sido use the same nickname bestowed on her first husband?)

Yet this image of the mutually obsessed, harmonious duo clashes with what Brunet, for example, asserts was the truth: Sido's favourite child was Achille. Colette suffered from violent jealousy, he tells us, and this was one solution, to deny it by putting herself in the forefront of the family portrait, capturing and holding Sido's maternal gaze, and pushing her siblings into the background. Though in Sido she names Achille 'the unrivalled firstborn', she does not pursue this thread. It is Brunet who asserts that Sido's jealous possessiveness of Achille allowed her to pursue him to Châtillon-sur-Saone, where he had settled following his marriage, taking the family with her (SVV 12).

To complete writing this chapter I have reread *La Maison de Claudine* several times, scanning to and fro, omitting certain chapters in favour of others. I have permitted myself to concentrate on the particular aspects I find compelling. I have discovered I needed to dwell on the overarching image of Sido, the mother. I now see her as a far more complex character than I did formerly. That mirrors, to some extent, how my view of my own mother has changed over the years, as I have gone on thinking about her, trying to understand her better, see her point of view. I have moved from a childish need either to idealize her or to see her as a tyrant to recognizing the difficulties in her life—for example, surviving the war as a French *assistante* teacher in Wales, cut off for five years from her family in occupied France (a German soldier billeted in the family cottage), losing her first child when he was three days old, becoming a mother caring for four children while also working full-time, sometimes feeling trapped by suburban life, not having much money, which made her way of coping turn her into someone stern and distant. She learned to survive by repressing her emotions. She found it very difficult when I did not repress mine. I certainly yearned to be her favourite but knew I was not. I can sympathize with Colette spinning her golden version.

I conclude that the more often I reread *la Maison de Claudine*, the more problematic and fascinating I find it. That makes me want to go back to it and read it yet again. Every time I do, it both grips and escapes me. It is a shapeshifter of a book.

In fact, it describes a shapeshifter of a house.

Feminist readings of romantic thrillers in the Victorian Gothic tradition (taking their lead from literary masterpieces such as *Jane Eyre*, which in turn took its lead from earlier literature) point out that the plot is often activated by the dark, rambling, menacing house in which the action occurs. The surrounding bleak, wild landscape mirrors the emotional landscape of the hero or heroine.

A classic plot may turn on the discovery of a secret room. This often stands as a topographical image of the unconscious, a container for repressed energies and desires struggling for expression, or for repressed memories of shameful or forbidden acts. In female Gothic, these are often wife murder, adultery, incest, rape, infanticide. Fantasies and fears become embodied in madwomen in attics or corpses in cellars. The discovery of the secret room is a narrative moment that dramatically changes the reader's view of the house, from initially welcoming to threatening.

Something similar seemed to be happening with the houses Colette describes in *La Maison de Claudine*. The secret room I discovered as I read expands to become both a whole series of secret rooms and indeed a secret house. I felt amazed, and then foolish, when I realized, only on my most recent rereading, that (in a reversal of the order of events in the classic Gothic tale) the dark, gloomy, half-ruined mansion-in-the-forest of Sido's first marriage, presented by Colette as a vast, cold, isolated semi-dungeon surrounded by swamps and woods, far away from civilization, is in fact also the very same warm, light-filled, bustling village house, set in a main street, full of domestic and intellectual creativity, of her second. They are precisely the exact same building. Colette has waved her magic pen-wand and transformed one into the other.

Perhaps I should say that she has superimposed one on the other. They nudge up against each other, change places, in a play of shadow and light. For me, the house of the early story goes on haunting the house of the later one. In this latest reading of mine, the 'good' house is simultaneously the 'bad' one, and the footsteps of the lost daughter sound overhead in the attic.

I have allowed this chapter to become so long because it introduces and explores the important figure of the mother, establishing Sido as that maternal emblem: Colette's inspiration; the core of my rereading of Colette. Now I shall look at ways in which that maternal image is refracted in other works by Colette.

2

MOTHER REMEMBERED

Sido's vital presence, behind, below, and inside the text, also helps form *La Naissance du jour* (1928), published in English in Enid McLeod's translation, with the title *Break of Day*, in 1961. Where *La Maison de Claudine* is a memoir constructed and written like a piece of fiction, *Break of Day* is a novel infused with autobiography.

The theme of maternal influence becomes immediately clearer when I retranslate the book's original title as *Birth of Day*. Now I become alert to the novel's central meditation on different kinds of birth, tugging various linked meanings from that one primal experience. As the meanings are born, so they pile up in layers of metaphor: the birth of day; the birth of a daughter; the birth of sensuality and thought; the birth of moral growth.

Colette, naming herself as narrator, the maker of novels, simultaneously emphasizes her overlapping identity as her mother's daughter, and muses on the gifts afforded to her by being born of, made by, that particular woman, Sido. Colette's novel, her gift to us, is, we discover as we read it, also born of Sido, in that it is inspired by her. The gift of life includes the gift of maternal knowledge, of maternal example.

The widowed Sido, we learn, remains brave, active, and independent. In her village home in Burgundy, she is an early riser, cherishing those moments at the end of night just before redness begins to streak the sky. In Provence, as the novel opens, her wakeful daughter in her own small house copies her by waking early. This shared relish for the approach of morning deepens their loving connection, particularly as Colette is sharing with the reader one of Sido's letters and musing about her with renewed tenderness and admiration.

The novel is crucially marked, formed, by shifts in time, those that construct the narrative and those alluded to by the narrator. So, in this first chapter, for example, the narrator Colette, in the present, evokes the past, when her mother wrote her the letter she cites, and also the future: the day just about to dawn; a possible visit from her mother's ghost. Pre-dawn darkness, glimmering with the promise of light, makes possible a psychological kind of birth. The moments before dawn become a time for thinking, for reverie, for memories of sexual and maternal love, for change. A liminal space; a liminal time. These minutes tremble with the possibility of transformation, of new adventures and discoveries. They exist in non-linear time, in a world of imagination and maternal holding not ruled by the ticking of seconds and minutes.

Read on the level of story, the novel is a beguiling account of a middle-aged woman spending some hot summer weeks in her house near St Tropez in the south of France, relishing the sensual pleasures offered by sun and sea, enjoying the company of friends and admirers for food and wine, for conversation and dancing. Drama is supplied by a tug of war between an older and a younger woman, simultaneously between sexual desire and sexual renunciation. However, the novel cannot be reduced to its plot. Rather, read like a musical script, it functions as a psalm of praise with a complex melody and phrasing, key repetitions; a psalm offered to life, to the life force.

The theme of birth suggests an image of metaphor itself. Metaphor links previously unrelated things by saying simply this is that. Just as inner feelings move outside a person when they are expressed in the imagistic language that already exists in the world, that therefore connects inner and outer worlds, so the unborn child leaves the mother, is born, and is given meaning by her. You are me becomes you are not me, and for a while both statements seem true and overlap. Mother and child, once a unity, learn to separate psychologically as well as physically. Colette's novel forms a meditation on this process and shows that it is recurrent. Persephone leaves and returns, leaves and returns.

In Colette's version, the narrative of natural, biological time is disrupted: birth can happen in adulthood. Honouring the lively memory of her mother, the narrator is born into a new stage of her life as a result of embracing loss as well as fullness, renunciation as well as fulfilment. The novel traces and enacts the paradox that death is necessary for life. Loving the mother who gave birth to you, meditating on her, helps you see that.

Birth of Day reads like a psalm, yes, but also like a love song to Sido, a love poem. Letters from Sido, the one at the beginning already mentioned and another one at the end, enclose and brace the text. A maternal holding. Quotations from others of Sido's letters interleave the story. A complex mutual involvement is enacted: the daughter's writing embodies and contains the mother's; the mother's writing, quoted, caresses the daughter, the daughter's text. Glosses it. Glossing a text, we stroke it; caress its feline fur.

Colette addresses her mother directly throughout. Sido is dead, we learn on the first page, but it is hard to believe and remember that as we read on. Her warm, living presence does not haunt the text so much as animate it. Sido is reborn in Colette's memory and imagination. At the same time, Sido gives birth to her daughter again, this time as a fully fledged writer rather than a beginner.

The novel, crucially concerned with maternal and sexual bodies, is itself a body, an active linguistic one, alive and dancing with words. It embodies, shows, a process of becoming: a woman breaks from the chrysalis of the past and becomes her new self; the writer breaks from traditional literary forms and constructs a new sort of novel. *Birth of Day* has a revolutionary form, which Colette had to invent. This new form is necessary, crucial, so that Colette can say what she needs to. New bottles for new wine.

How does she do it? How does she enable herself to break out of old forms? She lets herself be inspired by others' writing. In this case, Sido's letters, which, as we know from Claude Pichois's introduction to the Flammarion paperback edition of *La Naissance du jour*, Colette reread before starting to compose. Colette makes clear that this rereading confronted her with her mother's intellectual legacy, her Fourieresque philosophy of re-evaluating the passions. She addresses Sido directly: 'I haven't got the blind security with which you delightedly examined "good" and "evil", nor your art of re-baptizing according to your code certain poisoned old virtues and certain poor sins that had been waiting for centuries to belong in paradise' (*LNJ* 85; *BD* 66).

Is Colette's statement of lack really true? I have always seen her writing as possessing that 'security', that 'art', in a fundamental way. Perhaps she found that those qualities have to be constantly sought, constantly practised. Perhaps they coexist in tension with the wish for comforting certainties, the wish to ignore certain ambiguities. A good writer has to push past the desire for oversimple characterization and answers and courageously find the language to express and explore confusion, troubling thoughts, and subjects. At any rate, acquiring or reacquiring that confidence from Sido, learning or relearning Sido's skill in reappraisal, Colette frees herself to write *Birth of Day*, which upturns certain received wisdoms about goodness, ageing, and desire.

Colette knows that she is popularly considered to write about the 'felicity and discord' of love, assumed to be the core of a woman's being. She ripostes: 'the catastrophe of love, its consequences, its phases, have never been, at any time, part of the real intimate life of a woman.' A woman writing about love, she warns us, throws her watchers off guard. They follow the beam of her searchlight and ignore the encircling shadows, where something else altogether may be going on. Colette insists that she is trying to explore female subjectivity, composed of 'confused and important secrets, which she herself does not understand very well' (*LNJ* 81; *BD* 62). Rather than rehashing old dilemmas, she is a revolutionary, venturing into the unknown.

Colette would develop this thought in the opening of *Bella Vista* (1937),[1] when she stated that it was absurd to believe that periods in a woman's life empty of love affairs should be labelled 'blanks'. She might have been simply resisting a sexist assumption that men matter supremely, but I read her as implicitly suggesting that, when a woman is with a man, the story is to some extent a given; dictated by culture and history. The white pages, on the other hand, are exhilaratingly open. The woman has to write her own story, invent it for herself. Colette relished the opportunities offered by gaps, as we saw above in the form she invented for *La Maison de Claudine*.

Birth of Day describes a woman who is without a man and invents a new kind of form to express this 'blank', these white pages. It combines fiction, autobiography, memoir, reverie, letters. Nowadays when discussing this sort of literary mixing we use the terms postmodernism and autofiction. Colette's originality of invention predates such terms. Labelling can fence off a work before I have tried it for myself, can guide my response. If I need to label this text of Colette's, I see her as an experimental modernist, showing us how her work is made: she comments on what she has just written, she questions the reader, she consults with Sido's ghost. She may pretend from time to time that she is artless, just idly daydreaming and free-associating, but her *roman fleuve* demonstrates a sophisticated handling of narrative. She plays not only with time structures, as I mentioned above, but also with imagery. Remembered phrases from Sido's letters float across the text as they float across Colette's memory, acquiring deeper resonance with each repetition. For example, in one letter Sido describes sitting back and watching her neighbour's barn take fire and burn. She loves a good fire, a good disaster. Since the barn was filled only with straw, she emphasizes, she can safely enjoy the spectacle. Later, Colette repeats Sido's image—'it was only straw'—three times at different moments in her story, to refer wryly to human passions flaring up and dying down. Colette observes these as detachedly as Sido does the fiery show. Sido blazes up each time in Colette's memory, indestructible as a phoenix. Her letters are similarly indestructible.

As I have said, *Birth of Day* opens with a quotation from one of these letters. Sido is writing to Colette's unnamed then husband

(Henri de Jouvenel), who has invited her to come and visit the couple. Sido demurs. Her pink cactus, which only flowers once every four years, is about to bloom, and she must not miss it. She is old, and close to death, and this will be her last chance to witness a longed-for sight. The text then erupts into a hymn of triumph, a heretical Magnificat, in which Colette seems to throw her arms wide as she praises her mother:

> I am the daughter of a woman who, in an inferior, mean, narrow-minded country district, opened her village house to stray cats, tramps, and pregnant servants. I am the daughter of a woman who, desperate twenty times over at her lack of money for others, went out under the wind-whipped snow crying from door to door of the rich that a child had just been born into an impoverished household possessing no baby linen, naked into defeated naked hands … May I never forget that I am the daughter of that woman who leaned, trembling, over the spikes of a cactus, her wrinkled face dazzled at the prospect of a flower, that woman who herself never ceased to bloom, indefatigably, for three quarters of a century. (*LNJ* 20; *BD* 6)

Sido is magnificently resurrected by her daughter's quotation of her words. The chapter, having hinted at the narrator's own ageing, her own relish of life lived fully, ends on a whirl of metamorphosis, on a climax, on a metaphor for climax. Colette imagines her mother returning as a ghost, just as her daughter's lover slips away at dawn:

> 'Move aside, let me see', my beloved revenant will say. 'Ah! Surely that's my pink cactus that's survived me, and that you're embracing? How much it has grown and changed! … Stay there, don't hide yourself, I'd like the two of you to be left alone in peace, you and that one you're embracing, for I see that he is, in truth, my pink cactus, which is finally willing to bloom.' (*LNJ* 21; *BD* 7)

In her reverie, Colette fuses herself with her mother, a man with a plant, orgasm with flowering, in a magical, comic jouissance. All this in just two and a half pages.

But what is this novel actually about? you may ask.

Difficult question. How can I say what a novel is about? It is itself. Is it about Colette herself? Colette warns us against reading it as pure autobiography: 'do you imagine, as you read this, that I'm creating a self-portrait? Be patient: this is simply my model' (*LNJ* 19; *BD* 5). What does she mean here by her use of *modèle*? That she is making a representation? Just one possible version? She wraps the novel about us. We have to enter it and take it on her terms, and if we do that, the problems vanish.

We have to let ourselves be beguiled. Seduced into the land of the imagination, into a part of Provence where garden merges with beach, sea with sky. The wakeful Colette watches, thinks, fantasizes. She draws us in to share her night-time reverie, which skims back and forth in time but which constantly returns to images of other summer nights in the south of France, also to nights that Sido has previously witnessed and described. We enter Colette's world via her evocation of night-time sounds that she hears from her ground-floor bedroom: the creak of the cicadas, an insect crushing tiny bits of grit between its shards, a bird calling in the pine tree.

Night melts into day, the mood shifting into the dreaminess of what Colette names a second sort of 'night', the after-lunch siesta. The present swiftly becomes the future, as Colette imagines hearing the clink of the bottles being carried to the well to cool before dinner. 'One of them, red-currant pink, will accompany the green melon; the other … amber-coloured … goes with the salad of tomatoes, pimentos and onions, and with the ripe fruit' (*LNJ* 23; *BD* 8). These musings proceed by free association, looping and leaping. Colette begins thinking of other tasks: 'After dinner I mustn't forget to irrigate the ... melons, and to water ... the balsams, phlox and dahlias, and the young tangerine trees.' Time flows further on: 'Tomorrow, I'll surprise the red dawn on the tamarisks wet with salt dew, on the mock bamboos, a pearl tipping each blue lance' (*LNJ* 23; *BD* 8).

Day, with its sunlit brilliance, needs the indigo shades of night. The novel's descriptions of daytime encounters with friends and neighbours balance them against the summoning of beloved presences at nightfall; both the living and the dead. The novel's main action occurs both in light and in shadow. Its climactic scene, the difficult conversation between Colette and the young man in love with her, lasts through a single night. The birth of day brings resolution.

This is an intensely sensual novel, striking particularly for its powerful evocations of the mixed smells composing different aspects of the landscape: eucalyptus and over-ripe peaches, a hot, vinegary, aromatic bath, melon rinds floating on the water of the port, coarse tobacco and green mint, sandalwood, clothes soaked in brine. A fig tree smells of milk and flowering grass. Wine gives off a warm vapour. A blonde woman, burnt terracotta-red by the sun, perspiring, has her own distinctive scent. The smell of the sea combines with that of grilled chickens and myrtle.

But the characters? Who are the characters?

First of all, there is Colette herself, that is to say the self-image she tilts towards us, which constantly changes, depending on whom she is with and whom she is addressing. By turn, as the story develops, she manifests herself as Sido's adoring daughter, as Madame Colette the famous writer, as a talented cook, as an ardent gardener mulching her newly planted tangerine trees with seaweed, as a femme fatale and love rival of a younger woman, as a friend, as the ex-lover of un-numbered men. Then there is her young neighbour, Vial, an interior designer, who is in love with her, and Hélène, a would-be artist, who is in love with Vial. Around them tumbles a supporting cast of painter friends, male and female, who gather in the evenings to eat together on vine-hung terraces, to gossip and drink and dance in seaside bars.

The core of the book is the long scene between Colette and Vial, when they stay up all night talking. *Une nuit blanche*, a white night when you do not sleep, usually refers to a night of lovemaking, but in this case the two protagonists hardly touch physically. They fence with words, they feint, dodge, draw back, plunge forward again. The climax of the scene involves Colette renouncing her sexual interest in Vial, heroically letting go of him, pushing him towards Hélène. Vial resists Colette's efforts: 'you want to tell me that Hélène Clément loves me, that my indifference saddens her, that I should take pity on her and even love this "beautiful sane young girl" and marry her? Good. I know that. That's the end of it. Let's not talk of it again' (*LNJ* 120; *BD* 98). In the end, though, he yields to Hélène. Is he lazy? Conventional and bourgeois? Colette does not spell it out. She simply reveals that the marriage plot wins. Vial and Hélène are written off.

The characters' vacillations, towards each other and away, towards possible futures and away, are re-enacted in the book's shifts in time, darting back and forth between present and past. Colette's reverie holds everything gently and loosely, her looping, circling, darting free associations making the book a *roman fleuve*, while at the same time Colette senses herself as held eternally in her mother's reverie, in her mother's own free associations.

Maternal time, as I have said above, is not ordinary time. Rereading her mother's letters, Colette seems to be narrating from inside them, held by them, and also from outside them, as she holds them and scans them. Putting the letters into the narrated context of her own life gives them new meanings.

Rereading *La Naissance du Jour*, I salute it yet again as a brilliantly original work, born of writerly necessity, aesthetic necessity. Michèle Sarde likens Colette, in this respect, to one of the existentialists, who, 'rather out of fashion now, have noted the act of freedom that precedes the act of writing'. Sarde goes on to quote Sartre writing on Genet: 'genius is not a gift, but rather the way out one invents in desperate situations' (CFF 8). I read *La Naissance du Jour* as Colette's feeling compelled to meditate on her culture's contempt for older women, assumed to be kindly stay-at-homes, also assumed to be sexless, not to require erotic love. Written with urgency and passion, *La Naissance du Jour* resists this, by making Sido capable of enjoying destruction and 'a good disaster', and by making Colette the object of the much younger Vial's desire.

Claude Pichois takes a more prosaic view of the novel's genesis than I do. He considers that Colette was simply working to a deadline. She had promised Flammarion a novel, and was therefore obliged to write one, since she needed money, and novels paid well. He seems to think it a failure as a novel, quoting Andre Billy's review in *L'Œuvre* of 17 April 1928: '*La Naissance du Jour* is not a novel, although it has all the exterior character of one.' Pichois quotes Colette's polite thanks to Billy: 'one can hide nothing from your clear-eyed judgement: you have sniffed out that in this novel there was no novel at all' (*LNJ* 7). I wonder what Colette really felt as she wrote that?

Pichois continues: 'the novel does not exist, because it was impossible for it to do so.' With what confidence he lays down the literary law! With what arrogance! The reason for the novel's non-existence, apparently, is that it hesitates, formally, 'between the novel, a rhapsody about the Mediterranean landscape and summer friendships, the evocation of personal love affairs, old and new, and a memorial to Sido that a secret duty obliged [Colette] to erect'. He cannot recognize or praise Colette's groundbreaking invention. A hundred years later we can.

Pichois has a second problem with the novel. He finds the character of Vial 'unconvincing' but does not spell out why. Colette certainly found writing that central renunciation scene tricky. Pichois quotes her writing to her close friend Marguerite Moréno: 'I've re-begun my scene with the man *eight* times.' Pichois adds: 'if Colette had begun it sixteen times it would be no more convincing.' He thinks that not just Vial but Colette's male characters in general lack life: 'It's as though they are crushed by a masculine presence in Colette's own life' (*LNJ* 8). In this particular case, the 'masculine presence' was apparently Colette's third husband, Maurice Goudeket. Goudeket himself repudiated the idea that he inspired anything in the novel. Pichois quotes him as saying 'I am not the model [for Vial], as has been thought, and could never be' (*LNJ* 8).

I have no problem at all with the character of Vial. Rather than criticizing him for not living up to some time-bound norm of maleness, for not being 'realistic', I am more interested in Colette's portrayal of him as a version of a type she employs in other novels such as *Chéri* (discussed in my next chapter), the handsome, sulky, lost boy, who can be moulded by a loving older woman, quasi-maternal, into someone acceptable and civilized. Part of the erotic game, the erotic dance, is the wrestling between them that goes on. Yes, the power battle that Judith Thurman sees Colette engaging in so often, that reignites desire.

Vial is believable simply because he is the narrator's powerful fantasy, compellingly drawn. Tongue-tied and unwillingly polite, he is seen mainly from the outside. The novel is remarkable in that it makes considerable space for the female gaze. For an older woman's gaze. Colette spends a fair of bit of time peeping at handsome Vial half-naked in his brief swimming trunks or daydreaming or asleep. She watches him with a connoisseur's eye, appreciating his brown skin, his build. Perhaps Pichois finds that disconcerting?

Pichois also absurdly scolds Colette for writing a novel of sexual renunciation while not actually living that out herself. Having met Goudeket, fifteen years her junior, she had embarked on a blissful affair with him. Pichois quotes Colette writing to Renée Hamon, in the same letter to Hamon I have already mentioned, in which Colette gives her young friend advice on writing: 'you don't write a love story while you're making love.' Pichois follows this with the sour riposte: 'but the reverse: writing a novel of renunciation while making love is not true.' Turning someone beloved 'who is graced with all the seductions of life' into someone whom one renounces does not work, he insists (LNJ 8). Well, I believe Goudeket that he was not the model for Vial.

Pichois notes that, when La Naissance du Jour appeared, Colette was 54 years old. This is 'the moment when she passes from maturity into a vigorous old age'. Therefore, he insists, 'she should be writing a novel of renunciation. But she renounces renunciation.

One only writes about the past. She is living the present. Accordingly, she writes a poem of renunciation, to avert the future that menaces her and to protect this autumnal love that attaches her to Maurice Goudeket' (*LNJ* 10). Convoluted logic! Pichois seems to be suggesting that the novel is a magic spell, whereby Colette protects herself from having to imagine her love affair with Goudeket ending. What amuses me in Pichois's interpretative contortions is his assumption that Colette, at 54, is old, and should not be thinking of love. I know that in his day women were assumed to lose their sexual allure early on. Colette's narrator herself acknowledges this. She gazes at herself unflinchingly in the mirror, seeing herself as a Pichois would see her. Is that the only way for her to be seen? Am I a freak? In my early seventies I have not lost my interest in eroticism, my appetite for new adventures. According to Pichois I should have given up twenty years ago.

La Naissance du Jour shows Colette renouncing Vial, so that Hélène can have him, but in the context of the novel overall that is a minor renunciation. Colette can give him up, because she has so often possessed him with her eyes, her memory, her imagination. She can let go of him, all the while relishing her sensual appreciation of his charm and beauty, as she knows she will eventually let go of this little house in this enchanting Provençal landscape, as St Tropez turns into a hectically busy, crowded, noisy resort, and as she knows she has already let go of her beloved mother. The novel's playing with time, coiling and zigzagging, expresses how the things we let go of in reality return to us in our imaginations as treasures of our deep selves, never to be lost. As I write, I am selling my little house in France, because my life has changed, and I go there far less to write than I formerly did, and also it seems immoral to own a house I hardly live in any more. Also, a fact

Colette would approve of my taking into account: I can no longer afford to keep it on. Yet, inspired by Colette, I know that I shall keep it in my memory, always cherish what it has given me.

The novel ends with Colette quoting from the last letter she received from Sido, in which Sido lets go of 'the obligation to employ our language. Two pencilled sheets bear nothing more than apparently joyful signs, arrows emerging from a sketched word, little rays, two "yes, yes", and a "she danced", very clear' (*LNJ* 167; *BD* 142).

Sido renouncing conventional language, conventional meaning, inspires her daughter to begin writing her novel. The ending loops back to the beginning. Death enables life. The novel, written in the shape of a spiral, reaches forwards, into new life, planting seeds of admiration and reverence in the reader. Yes, yes, I say with Sido. This acquiescence on my part is an internal bowing-down to the book, an internal gesture of recognition, a powerful physical experience of pleasure and satisfaction, made in silence.

Now comes the struggle to articulate why I make this strong salute. It is a recognition of beauty: what seems to me formal perfection, newly and differently invented and designed, harmonious correspondences of balance and proportion that change and dance; a warm, living body. *La Naissance du Jour* seems—exactly right.

First of all, in this rereading of Colette, I looked at how a daughter, in full daughterly mode, regarded and remembered her mother. Next, I have looked at how a daughter, acknowledging her own adulthood, balances her view of herself against lively memories of her mother. Now, I propose to look at how the image of the mother can play across adult desire and love.

3

MOTHER REFOUND
AND REJECTED

Chéri (1920) is a short, compact novel, set just before the First World War. It explores the changing relationship and power play between Léa, a wealthy Parisian courtesan, and her boyfriend-gigolo, the eponymous Chéri, half her age, whom she keeps, cherishes, and finally discovers she loves. The blurb on the back of my Penguin copy (the 1930 translation by Roger Senhouse)[1] calls it Colette's 'most famous and perhaps her finest book'. That may well be objectively true, but I remember being disturbed by *Chéri* when I first read it, in my twenties. I retained an impression of a decadent confection, some kind of soft, sugary, pale pink meringue wrapped in pale pink tissue paper, adorned with a pink satin bow.

How glad I am to have given it another chance. Rereading *Chéri* recently in order to review a new translation, I read it very differently.[2] Colette herself, as I have mentioned above, recommended looking for a long time at what we like and even longer at what we do not like. Prodded by her, I found that the novel raised topics that in my own writing I regularly felt urgent about exploring, even if they also upset me: for example, female rivalries; women exchanging sexual favours for money; bad mothers.

I changed my mind about *Chéri*. I discovered that the novel now spoke to me in ways it had not done before and that I had plenty to say back to it. Ostensibly a tragi-comedy of brittle manners, it is also, I decided, an exploration of the development of a self. Now I noticed that language, both spoken and descriptive, formed not only the novel's materiality but also its subject. The novel describes a birth. Not multiple kinds of birth, as in *Birth of Day*, but a singular one: a young man's delayed, eventual birth into adult language and the rules and regulations of the world that language describes.

The theme of disobedience/obedience, key to the drama, is hidden at first. There are plenty of other felicities to admire. Rereading *Chéri*, this time in French, has been a revelation of Colette's powers of characterization and scene-setting, her deft, sharp dialogue, her wit, her acute observation.

Since the novel concerns a woman who has made a living from selling her sexual skills, it opens appropriately in her luxurious bedroom in her big house in the Parisian suburbs. Morning. Two lovers. One still languishing in bed and the other posing in front of a mirror. Colette creates a voluptuous world of sensual experience, plunging us straight into it and then disconcerting us, just as sex can do. The narrative perspective zigzags engagingly, offering abrupt changes of perspective in the same way that a cubist painting does. Along with avoiding steady narrative authority, the novel will disclaim conventional moral judgements. My account of the novel is similarly cubist, darting back and forth over and underneath scenes and images, juxtaposing images separated by several pages in the original, constructing my own sense of it. It is an active way of reading that the novel invites. To write this account of it I have happily reread it several times, each time finding new emphases.

This opening scene has Chéri defying traditional masculine codes by decking himself with Léa's massive pearl necklace and claiming it suits him much better than her. The male gaze here does not objectify the female but is resolutely narcissistic, as Chéri preens himself in the mirror and demands admiration. The female gaze remains dispassionate, Léa watching her lover tear open his pyjama jacket the better to reveal his chest 'curved like a shield' and the pearls lying against it. All we see of Léa are her upraised arms, those arms that signify her holding and enfolding of Chéri, which is the core of the novel. Certain details of the setting are provided by a more distanced narrator. We get a momentary flash—no more—of Chéri's inner world. The reader is pulled in, at first a welcomed voyeur peeping at the bedroom, the bed, and then Léa's privileged confidante as she observes her young lover with wryly intelligent indulgence. The role reversal of the game they are playing with the pearl necklace alerts us to another, to do with age: whereas it might be considered normal in western culture for an older man to take up with a younger woman, here we are watching an older woman take up with a boy.

The drama is so powerful, the tension between Léa and Chéri so compelling, that I found it easy to glide over Colette's polished sentences, to rush past what her words are actually doing and saying. Accordingly, rereading a second and third time, I slowed down, and attended to the novel's language far more than formerly. Once I did this, I became aware of just how supple and muscular the prose is, and admired the devices Colette uses to move the story along, in terms not just of the actions of characters but also of the narrative, sentence by sentence. The book feels physical and alive; something is breathing under the surface of the text. No. I have put that clumsily, suggesting that text is hard, like a lid, keeping the subtext down. I want to say that the narrative, the novel's body, is like fertile earth after rain, full of life, stirring with unseen energies and currents of meaning. The images, such as the flesh-pink walls of the bedroom, the nipple-like pearls, are not decorative but integral, organic. They structure a secret story that is at the same time in plain view. They point to it.

What is the explicit story about? Love and loss, I would say. Anything else? Henri de Jouvenel, Colette's second husband, a journalist and politician, used to get impatient with Colette's concentration on these subjects, deeming them frivolous. He was the frivolous one, taking and discarding mistresses at whim, even after marrying Colette, expecting her to condone his affairs and not express jealousy. Assuming his entitlement to sexual conquest, he did not feel obliged to analyse his behaviour. Male-defined politics, the power play between men, mattered more than self-knowledge and reflection. Women were necessary for a man's pleasure and relaxation, but their concerns did not affect or interest him. He took for granted the traditional split between the outer world of high finance and chambers of deputies, seen as a crucially male domain, and the inner one of domesticity and relationships, accepted as lesser because connected to women. Colette crashes through this distinction. Her novel shows how the two worlds are interdependent. The sexual politics at play in the bedroom are intertwined with financial interests and calculation. An ageing courtesan, her value as a commodity diminishing, simply switches from selling herself to trading in stocks and shares. A dull, timid young woman is worth marrying because she is rich. The amoral underworld props up the hypocritical high-bourgeois one.

Anyway. Love and loss, then, yes. Experienced in what kind of landscape? The book's setting offers a clue to the secret story.

Chapter 1 opens in Léa's bedroom, as I said above. An opulent, richly decorated interior space, warm and comfortable. The walls are rose-pink. Léa's wide wrought-iron bed is decorated with incised copper—a rich pink-gold glow. The sun burnishes this metal nest as it pierces through the pink curtains, casting a rosy light on the interior of the room, rippling over the pale frills of bedlinen and lace. The sun sparkles on Chéri's white teeth, the whites of his eyes, the white pearls of Léa's necklace with which he is playing. Léa's gleaming bed reminds me of an open, iridescent oyster shell, pink-fleshed Léa in her mature beauty forming the pink pearl inside. The bed displays her, as she knows very well, blue-eyed and smiling, long-legged and voluptuous. The intensity of the morning sunlight burning through the curtains produces dramatic contrasts. Chéri, his dark hair blue-tinged like a blackbird's plumage, prances in front of the curtains, 'all black, like a graceful devil against a blazing furnace' (Ch. 7; CFC 15). Then, when he steps back towards the bed, he becomes all white again, from his silk pyjamas to his Moroccan slippers.

The chapter brims with other sorts of sensual detail, such as the splashing of bathwater, the softness of skin, the smoothness of the pearls, the silk upholstery of the antique chairs. All these images combine to create the bedroom's intimate atmosphere and underline Léa's preoccupation with bodily pleasure and material comfort. We seem to be lolling blissfully on a billowy cloud.

Bliss is maintained by servants: the maid who runs Chéri's bath, picks up his clothes, and fetches his breakfast of hot chocolate and buttery brioches, the butler who selects the wine to accompany the exquisite lunch provided by the chef, the footman who polishes the wine glasses, the chauffeur who runs Léa about town. They know their places in the hierarchy and stay there. Léa knows her place, too, firmly fixed in the demi-monde: she has spent her life as a *grande horizontale*, subjugating her own desire in order to service men's sexual whims and so earn an excellent living. With savings heaped up in the bank, she can now relax with her young lover. He and she also occupy fixed positions: she is the older one, in command, who spoils her kept boy with presents, and he is the doted-upon, passive recipient of her cherishing. Their mutual teasing, as they pivot around each other, does not upset the balance of their relationship but keeps the top spinning. It is when Léa changes the rhythm, changes how she speaks, that the power dynamic shifts and things start to topple.

The secret story propelling the novel is fired by the energy of myth. I think that in *Chéri* Colette is creating her own version of the Christian myth of Paradise and Paradise Lost. She was taught the Christian stories as a child, as I said in Chapter 1, and this founding myth of the Christian religion seems to have stayed with her. It lends resonance and depth to her novel, gives it a strong shape. Whereas in *La Maison de Claudine* the myth glosses the ambivalences of the mother–daughter relationship, here Colette uses it to explore mother–son tugs of war.

At its beginning, light flooding into the pink bedroom, the novel evokes not just the start of a new day but the very start of the world. Before the Fall, everything in the Garden of Eden is harmonious. There is no painful division. Opposites are connected:

woman and man, darkness and light, hardness and softness, sound and silence, maturity and childhood. Even Heaven and Hell. (Later on, Léa will apostrophize Chéri as her beautiful demon, her fallen angel.) I have not got a language to evoke this state of non-division, because language divides things by naming them. Colette gains her effect by showing us, making the state of non-division visual; felt. On a deep level we are in a prelinguistic state, dandled inside a cocoon of simple being, of pleasure. A dream of infancy? The room holds the bed holds Léa holding Chéri. They embrace inside a shining iridescent bubble. Before it bursts, the narrator shows us, lingeringly, its fragile beauty.

Unity soon begins to break up. If I change my image and now see Léa's bed as a cocoon, I watch it crack open. Chéri is necessarily born from it, first into the flesh-pink room and thence, once he is dressed in his smart day clothes, into the courtyard, the street. He is off to lunch with his mother, Charlotte, and her friends, and Léa, an old sparring partner of his mother's, will join them afterwards.

The Biblical myth shows Adam and Eve as existing in the beginning in a state of innocence. Ignorance. They are named as man and woman, but sexual difference seems not to matter, and does not lead to desire and sexual action. It is their disobedience, the Fall, eating the forbidden apple of knowledge, that results in their becoming aware of their genitals and then feeling sexual desire. When Léa, relaxing opposite the dozing Charlotte sleeping off her lunch, reminiscences about her early relationship with Chéri, she remembers that theirs was initially an affectionate, sexless relationship. On one occasion, when she badgered him about his dissipated teenage lifestyle ruining his health, he responded disrespectfully, but his bad manners 'did not shock Léa, too intimate a friend, a kind of godmother out to spoil him whom he addressed with the familiar "tu"' (*Ch*. 30; *CFC* 31). Léa followed up this advice session soon afterwards, she remembers, with an explicit invitation. Remarking how pale and thin Chéri looks, she mentions that she is going away to the Normandy countryside, to her place near Honfleur, and offers to take Chéri with her, as a kind of convalescence for him: 'there'll be nothing to do but eat, drink, sleep … Good strawberries, fresh cream, tarts, little grilled chickens … Now there's a healthy diet, and no women!' Chéri leans against Léa's shoulder and closes his eyes: 'No women … great … Léa, you're a pal, aren't you? Yes? Right, let's be off. Women … I've had it with them' (*Ch*. 33; *CFC* 34).

She draws him closer and rocks him affectionately. When he commands her to kiss him, she touches her lips to his forehead, but he knots his arms around her neck and pulls her down to him for a kiss on the mouth.

No more pallyness. When Léa kisses him back, she does so with such passion that they reel apart, 'drunk, deafened, breathless, trembling, as though they had just been fighting'. Chéri is reduced to a childlike babbling: 'he murmured words, soft cries, a whole loving animal chant in which she made out her name, and "darling" "come here" "never leave you"' (*Ch*. 37; *CFC* 36).

Off they go to Normandy. The green, fertile countryside is presented in classic, Romantic terms as the epitome of wholesomeness, the opposite of the city with its decadence and ruinous temptations. Nature is bountiful, like a generous mother. Léa feeds her protégé with good, fresh food, watches him laze by the pond or dawdle along green alleyways. At night in their Eden they sleep together, Chéri's head on Léa's breast or nuzzled into her shoulder. Colette throws in casually, like an afterthought, that occasionally, on waking in the morning, they have sex. Sex is part of the purity of this secluded rural world.

Colette maps her version of the Adam and Eve story onto the Biblical one. She structures her narrative by simultaneously invoking Greek myth, the myth of Oedipus. She tells us an incest story. Judith Thurman has nodded to the incest theme of *Chéri*, I see from her biography of Colette, but I want to expand her mention and put the subject at the centre of my rereading.

The incest is metaphorical, obviously. Chéri names Léa his godmother. As an older woman, she scolds him, caresses him, instructs him, worries about his health, teases him. He laps it all up, as his due. She describes him to herself as her 'nursling', an image suggesting a child she has breastfed, now one she is bound to bring up properly. Once the two begin having sex, the incest goes on being metaphorical, of course, since Chéri is not Lèa's son. But they do seem to me to be acting out a joint dream of incestuous love and desire, initially veiled by denial. Léa, in Normandy, can watch the half-naked Chéri having his boxing lesson, can itemize and admire his beautiful physical traits, can try to fatten him up on a diet of corn-fed chicken and strawberries and cream, can assure herself that she feels 'happy and maternal, and bathed in tranquil virtue'. At the same time, she tells herself she feels indifferent. At the same time, she is sleeping with him. She taps his cheek, his leg, his thigh, with 'the irreverent pleasure of a wetnurse' (*Ch.* 7 46; *CFC* 42) Colette's text has *nourrice*. Roger Senhouse translates this as nanny. A *nourrice* is more than a nanny, in this context, I think.

It is spoken language that will eventually threaten the Eden in which Léa dandles Chéri. At the beginning of their affair, he does not confide in her when they are in bed together, unlike her previous young lovers. Colette employs a splendid cross-gender image to evoke this: 'he gave away nothing but his body, and remained as mysterious as a courtesan. Tender? Yes, if tenderness can infuse an involuntary cry, arms opened then closed. But as soon as he spoke, his "spitefulness" returned, his determination to reveal nothing.' Often, at dawn, after they have made love, she whispers to him, urging him to speak. 'But no avowal came from that arched mouth, and no words other than sulky or rapturous phrases.' These phrases are punctuated by cries of 'Nounoune', 'the name he had given her when he was small and which nowadays he called out in the depths of his pleasure, like a cry for help' (Ch. 47; CFC 43). *Nounoune* makes me think of *nounours*, a teddy bear. When I check with the dictionary, I find it comes from *nounou*, which Harrap's defines as a childish term derived from *nourrice*, giving childminder as a primary meaning and wetnurse as a subsidiary one. Chéri's usage might be translated 'Nursie'. Too comic and awkward? Let's stick to 'Nounoune', as Colette's translators do. It flags up, anyway, how in his sexual rapture in bed Chéri becomes again an infant. In his stubborn post-coital silence, he remains one. He hangs on to the delicious incestuous reunion with the mother figure. He wants to go on basking in its heady, taboo comfort, which is maintained by its speechlessness.

When he and Léa return to Paris after their Normandy idyll, they part, returning to their respective homes. But the very next night Chéri returns to Léa 'on silent winged feet … Undemonstrative, saying nothing, he was running towards her. They tumble into bed and make love. Chéri pretends to fall asleep, in order to grit his teeth and close his eyes, 'prey to a furious attack of taciturnity' (Ch. 49; CFC 43). Léa accepts his silence happily. She decodes the trembling of his body, certain that it spells out anguish, gratitude, and love.

If she is under an illusion, she sustains it cheerfully. She does not recognize it or investigate it. The relationship continues for seven years, centred in the refuge that is Léa's all-embracing bed. Outside bed, lolling around in the bedroom, Chéri continues being 'spiteful' and bantering, playing his role as Léa's 'wicked nursling'. She can deny her affection for him by speaking it as scolding. The novel begins its acceleration towards possible disaster when Chéri tosses out his spoken version of certain realities. In chapter 1, while he larks about and then gets dressed, he casually informs Léa of the forthcoming marriage into which his mother has urged him, and mocks the maternal jostling on both sides over the marriage settlements. He admits his relish of his own inherited fortune and the money he has saved by being kept by Léa. She acts unconcerned, bats his news aside, berates him tenderly.

In chapter 2, we leave the Garden of Eden, brimming with green plenty like a cornucopia, and enter instead its shadow version, the well-organized parklike grounds of the vast Neuilly villa where Chéri's mother, Charlotte Peloux, a rich, retired courtesan, holds sway over her court of toadies and hangers-on. Léa chooses to approach the house via this garden, with its trellised roses and clumps of rhododendrons in full blazing flower. I gain an impression of harsh, clashing colours and ugly shapes. I remember gardens like that from childhood visits to my grandparents in Normandy. One of the family's friends, a wealthy businessman, lived in a mansion near our village, and occasionally we were summoned there for tea. I remember the suffocating boredom of those afternoons in the dull house, the equally suffocating banality of the surrounding parklike garden with its ornamental evergreens dotting the vast swathes of green lawn set with the occasional bench. How could you suffocate in an open space? You could, if its showiness felt hostile. To me, as a child, a garden was ideally a wilderness into which you could plunge, inside which you could vanish as you explored it, out of sight of the authorities, but this sort of open-plan garden simply served as a spectacle; to indicate wealth and keep the hoi polloi at a distance. There was nothing to do in it except passively notice its size. The elderly owner wore a double-breasted suit and bow tie even in high summer, smoked cigars non-stop, and addressed females in his hoarse, rasping voice as doll. Why were my grandparents friends with him? No idea.

Colette describes a Paris on the sprawl. Madame Peloux's villa, once a country dwelling, is now simply yet another ornate residence in the outer suburbs. From the glass-walled garden room the lunch guests can admire the property's outhouses, converted stables, and kennels. Charlotte Peloux is the serpent who has tempted Chéri away from Léa in favour of attaching him to Edmée, the wealthy heiress, the shy, pretty daughter of yet another courtesan, Marie-Laure. Chéri will replace a relationship of which his mother jealously disapproves with one that is conventionally acceptable. If Léa plays the role of the Good Mother of the child's idealistic longing, meeting and fulfilling all his desires, Charlotte embodies the Bad one, who deprives the child of care. She has alternately ignored and adored her son, while abandoning him to the kitchen company of housemaids and menservants, alternately forgetting to feed him and stuffing him with sweets, and packing him off to a prison-like boarding school while she absconds with a lover; generally neglecting him. Of course he prefers Léa as a mother figure. Who wouldn't?

In the fallen, patriarchal world outside the heaven on earth of the incestuous boudoir, women survive as best they may. The Belle Epoque idealized and fetishized exaggerated femininity, while at the same time affording it a perverse, demonic side and according women few actual freedoms; female education was limited and female options constrained. Colette describes a society in which a woman has value only when deemed desirable to men. Accordingly, many women survive by selling themselves to those men, whether as prostitutes or as wives. Colette makes it clear that she links the two. Once over 50, a woman becomes what Léa herself, meditating on Chéri's imminent departure into marriage, calls 'a monster', disguising her disgustingness behind a screen of card games, good wine, bridge scorecards and knitting needles, 'all the trinkets required to stopper up a gaping hole' (Ch. 10; CFC 136). The hole refers to the lack of a male lover. It makes me think of a gaping vulva. Charlotte and Marie-Laure, and Léa too by implication, flounce and compete in a harem world, which has no room for loyalty and certainly not for the sisterhood believed in and hoped for by feminists. The relationship between Charlotte and Léa is characterized by Charlotte's bitchy remarks.

> They had known each other for twenty-five years. Hostile intimacy of light women whom one man enriches then casts aside and whom another man ruins, bad-tempered friendship of rivals on the alert for the other's first wrinkle or white hair. Camaraderie of practical women, adept at playing the money game, but one of them a miser and the other a pleasure-seeker. These bonds count. (Ch. 27; CFC 29)

Again, Colette foregrounds her characters' particular use of language as key to the drama. Léa can recognize and even relish Charlotte's needling, because she can fight back by pretending not to understand it. Open warfare will not do. Better to ignore the aggression inherent in the subtle insults. Her pride remains intact. Calm and humorous, she refuses to show hurt. Her skirmishes with Charlotte are comic, on one level, as she matches bitchy digs with clever ripostes, and grim on another, revealing how she cannot ever express how she feels. As a light woman, she has to take things lightly. Just as in her bedroom she presents only her best face to Chéri, denying any upset over the thought of losing him, remaining cheerful and unruffled, so in Charlotte's domain she refuses to give her antagonist the satisfaction of seeing her darts hit home. In my world, friends, if we unwittingly hurt each other, have to be tackled directly. William Blake was right. Friendship is worth the risk of telling our wrath. However, female friendship, the attendant struggle and celebration of equality, does not exist in Léa's world. Eve has no best friend.

In the terms of the biblical myth, the serpent–Charlotte, tempting Chéri with the acquisition of even more wealth represented by the dowry that Edmée will bring with her, first hinting and then emphasizing to Léa that her affair with Chéri must now end, helps destroy Léa's Edenic existence. (Edmée also recognizes Charlotte as an adversary, telling Chéri that the snake wriggling under the bedroom door is the truly dangerous creature.) Chéri departs on his honeymoon with Edmée, and Léa retreats to the south of France, pretending to take a new lover with her, in order to fend off Charlotte's triumphant crowing over her loss.

Once back in Paris, Chéri abandons his disappointing, too young wife and plunges back into the dissipated lifestyle of his youth. He discovers that drink, drugs, and women for sale are not actually what he wants. A wanderer seeking a refuge, he surveys the debauch from the sidelines. Then, one evening, wandering sadly past Léa's house, he sees that the lights are on. She has returned.

The lovers' reunion, Chéri bursting in on Léa late at night, is characterized at first by their habitual use of language. Léa scolds Chéri in her typical maternal fashion for arriving unannounced, and he sulks childishly. They spar, in brief, playacting sentences. Then Léa's unscrewing of the top of a scent bottle, the scent flooding Chéri, releases him into direct physical memory of pleasure, and he calls out to her twice: 'Nounoune'. This time, when she commands him, three times, to speak to her, he finally does so, crying out 'darling Nounoune! Darling Nounoune!' He collapses against her.

> Seated, she let him slip to the floor and sprawl against her with tears, disordered words—'Nounoune darling! I've found you again! My Nounoune! Oh Nounoune, your shoulder, and then your scent, and your necklace, my Nounoune, oh, it's wonderful,—and that little burnt taste your hair has, oh! It's—it's wonderful—'. (*Ch.* 159; *CFC* 118)

Léa berates him lovingly, and he stops babbling, listening to her with his head on her breast and begging for more if for one instant she halts her 'tender litany'. Finally, she holds him at arm's length and asks him 'so you loved me?' Chéri lowers his eyes 'in childish embarrassment: yes, Nounoune'.

He has never made this declaration before, and Léa realizes that she is close to abandoning herself to 'the most terrible joy of her life'. In return, a little later, she makes her own declaration: 'I haven't got a lover. I love you.'

Putting her love into words, she unwittingly courts danger. For the moment, they make love, and fall into the 'abyss' of simultaneous orgasm. Afterwards 'they remained entangled, and no words troubled the long silence of their return to life'. Chéri, preparing to fall asleep, murmurs in broken sentences his worries about what will happen the following day, and Léa soothes him tenderly: 'Don't worry. Lie down and sleep. Isn't Nounoune here? Don't think about anything. Sleep.' While he does so, Léa decides that they must go away together, escape Paris for somewhere peaceful and remote: 'I'll do the thinking for both of us—let him do the sleeping.' She cradles him. A dream troubles but does not wake him. Tenderly she calms him. 'She rocked him so that for a long time … he might go on resembling that "wicked nursling" never born to her' (Ch. 166; CFC 123).

The relationship can survive only as long as Léa combines the personae of mother and lover inside her flesh-pink, womblike bedroom. In the real world beyond, she has to face enemies such as Charlotte, reproaching her for keeping Chéri a bachelor for far too long and spoiling him for ordinary life, and potential enemies such as Chéri's deliciously young, pretty wife. For a while, musing overnight, Léa imagines she can win. However, her ecstatic fantasies of Chéri and herself openly becoming a couple, fleeing to the safe exile of the Riviera, mixing with tolerant, sophisticated compatriots who will accept their adulterous union, their age difference, are ruined next day by being converted into speech. Lea becomes a traditional Eve. It is all her fault! She brings about the Fall by eating the forbidden fruit, dreaming the forbidden dream, uttering the forbidden words. She ignores the taboo (the godlike instruction Chéri did not know he was going to uphold) forbidding incest to be witnessed and accepted in the outside world. Her losing her head and making her desire explicit is simultaneous with Chéri suddenly realizing that she is ageing. An older woman lover is all very well as long as she strives to hide her age with subtle make-up and flattering pale pink underclothes, but one who carelessly reveals her wrinkles is repulsive.

Clues to the forthcoming disaster pile up. First of all, on the morning following their reunion, Chéri wakes before Léa but feigns sleep so that he can watch her. No longer the softly accepting mother figure of dream, the sexy mother of enveloping night and scented darkness, she becomes simply a practical, organizing person examined in the bright, unforgiving light of day. She gets up briskly, consults a railway timetable, frowns in concentration. She pulls out a chequebook. It is all much too businesslike for Chéri. Now he notices disturbing signs: 'not yet powdered, a thin twist of hair on her nape, with a double chin and a ravaged neck, she was offering herself imprudently to his invisible gaze' (Ch. 170; CFC 125).

Chéri closes his eyes, tries to recapture the rose-pink bedroom 'as he saw it on the previous night, mysterious, the colour of the inside of a water melon, the enchanted dome of lamplight, and above all the exaltation with which he staggered under so much pleasure' (Ch. 171; CFC 126). In the novel's opening chapter, as I noted above, Léa lies in bed in the morning and observes Chéri, his black silhouette against the radiant curtains veiling the sun. In this final chapter, with Chéri separating himself from Léa, the perspective and the roles are reversed. Chéri lies in bed and observes Léa's black silhouette as she bustles about making her preparations for their departure. When she emerges into the light, she is not beautiful, as Chéri was in that early scene, but ugly.

Over breakfast, Chéri, struggling with his appalled realization of his changed perception of Léa, can think of nothing to say, but decides he will get away with it, since Léa knows he is always taciturn at this time. Misreading his silence for contentment, Léa blows it. She throws aside all her habitual caution, giving herself over to the pleasure of her avowal, finally being able to express what she feels without fear. She spills out her rapturous declaration. Chéri is her love, her great love, her only love. Dramatic monologue swiftly becomes grotesque comedy as she pauses without a breath to consider the letter to his wife that will have to be written, the luggage he will need, the yacht she will buy for them, the financial settlement to be made on Edmée. Grasping Léa's hand, Chéri notices its soft, flabby skin, its wrinkles. As he withdraws, she reaches for him, then faces reality. Courageously she realizes this is the end. Chéri may have come back, she tells him, but he has found 'an old woman'. Of course, therefore, she must let go of him. This prosaic admission in the terms of a sexist culture—old women are repulsive and cannot be desired—masks the recognition of another cultural taboo: sons must not have sex with their mothers.

Léa's recognition of cultural and moral reality marks the great shift in Chéri's use of language. Released from Léa's maternally/incestuously loving hold, Chéri abandons his former 'mutism' and unleashes torrents of speech. He is born into language. Into adult speech, which is ruled by the conventions of society. Whereas in bed he babbled, in what Julia Kristeva calls the semiotic, the infant's poetic murmurings and cries to the mother, now he enters the Symbolic, the grown-up word formulations dictated by patriarchy, the grammar of the Law of the Father. When Léa cannot stop herself from a jealous angry outburst at the thought of his returning to his wife, he tells her not to complain, to remain the 'chic type' she has always been, the chic type he loved at the beginning. 'If we've got to end it, did you have to go and be like other women?' He rushes on, telling her at great length how much he suffered during their separation, when he was first married and ran away from his wife, how he could think of nothing and no one but Léa, how much he missed her, the most beautiful, the best of women.

He has put Léa into a fixed, idealizing place in the rigidly organized grammar of his narrative. Now she belongs, not in the eternal present, dancing outside of time, of incestuous mother–child love, but in the past tense of male-ordered power relations: she used to be his lover. Stuck on her pedestal, like a sexlessly maternal Virgin Mary, Léa reacts with superb dignity, submitting to becoming merely a memory. She yields to the definition forced upon her. 'At the age when so many women have stopped living, I was for you the most beautiful, the finest of women, and you loved me? How I thank you, my darling' (Ch. 181; CFC 133).

Accepting they can no longer be lovers, she simultaneously spells out her maternal loss: 'you are breaking away very late from me, my wicked nursling, I've carried you next to me for too long, and now you have a burden of your own to carry: a young wife, perhaps a child.' She goes further, urging him to enjoy his youth, to find true passion with his wife. 'She loves you: it's her turn to tremble, she will suffer as a lover does and not like a perverse mother. You will speak to her as a master, but not as a capricious gigolo. Quick, quick, be off' (Ch. 2 184; CFC 135).

Whereas in *La Naissance du Jour* the older woman appears freely to renounce the younger man, to demonstrate her generosity and power through her capacity to stand back, gracefully to open her arms and release him, here we see Léa coerced, parroting the common-sense rules of the culture. The end of their liaison is marked by her abjection. I cannot read her subservience as ironically declared. I read it as accepted. Man is master of his wife in marriage. The mistress cannot be the equivalent of the Master. The mistress is blotted out. Chéri has suddenly grown up and will act out the Law of the Father.

What do I conclude? What has this rereading given me?

Not simply the secret, or not-so-secret incest narrative I have just sketched, but also a string of metaphors: the Garden of Eden is the maternal body, is the one the son longs for, is the dream of incest, is the Fall, is the impossible story that must be cut short. The novel reinscribes the Christian myth: Paradise is necessarily lost. It reinscribes the Oedipal myth: do not love your mother too much! Tears after bedtime will follow. Léa's tears, not Chéri's. The novel closes with him fleeing into the street, into the springtime 'like a man escaping from prison'.

The novel, for all it engages me with its exquisite writing, its sensuality and irony, makes me feel sad too. Under its charm, humour, and precise observation lies tragedy: Léa's loss of value, her loss of love, youth, beauty, and desirability in a world where patriarchal values define these terms. Part of the story's poignant force derives from Léa's attempting to ignore, if not defy, the rules defining proper femininity. In so doing she exposes them in all their constraining cruelty. On the level of social morality, an equal part of the story's force lies in the novel's return to the status quo. Sexual order is restored, and the rules against incest reinstated. Perhaps the inevitability of the ending offers a relief to the reader. Temptation, having been tasted and enjoyed, can be renounced. The carnival's over and normal life is resumed.

This normal life is founded on acceptance of economic and sexual inequality. On one level Colette could be seen as a brave realist. In Léa's milieu, female relationships are structured by distrust and hostility. Women's degraded place in this culture, their gaining value only via male favour, makes them viciously competitive with one another. They exchange spiteful digs disguised as compliments. They measure each other up like animals at a trade fair, judge each other as harshly as do the men buying them. Léa may coolly deflect Charlotte's flung barbs, joining in her game with amused detachment while privately noting her rival's vanished youth and beauty, but towards the bashful, sweetly pretty Edmée and her resplendently beautiful mother Marie-Laure she is merciless, concluding to herself that, while Edmée is a perfect foil to Marie-Laure, the latter must hate her nonetheless. The coldness and brutality of Léa's attitude, her assumption that mothers necessarily hate and envy their daughters, contrasts sharply with her adoration of her young male lover. She cannot admire and enjoy a young woman's beauty and freshness, which women in my world can do; she feels it as a threat, which of course, in her world, it is.

How different this is from the portrait Colette offers in *La Maison de Claudine* of the mother–daughter relationship. In the paradise that Colette describes herself inhabiting with Sido, the mother names her young daughter her jewelled golden treasure. A safe metaphor. Since they are not caught up in the cruel cash nexus of being commodities sold on the open market, mother and daughter can go on tenderly cherishing each other with openly expressed affection, pet names. However, as I concluded in Chapter 1, that image of the mother–daughter relationship was idealistic, oversimple, polished up. In *Chéri* Colette offers a glimpse of mother–daughter hatred, a rift that cannot be mended. I wonder whether my perceiving this unhealable wound informed my initial hostility to the novel back in my twenties? Much as I battled with my own mother I also simultaneously yearned for her love and to be reconciled with her. Perhaps I just could not bear the coldness of Léa's world, in which that could not happen.

It is a truism that love and hate intertwine, that ambivalence is normal. However, ambivalence can feel hard to sustain if you are romantic and only want to believe in love. In my twenties I struggled with this. While I repudiated the romantic historical novels by Georgette Heyer that had gripped me in my early teens, which were basically survival guides to winning rich prizes in the marriage market, and while I criticized marriage as solely to do with property and male privilege, I still fell in love and still wanted to believe I could find a soulmate. At the same time I wanted to combat the prevalent view that women were easily catty and bitchy towards each other, that such behaviour was quintessentially feminine. I wanted to believe that women could be unfailingly sisterly, loyal, loving, and equal. At some level I was still in the grip of Catholic morality: good women versus bad women. It took me years to realize that goodness and badness coexisted inside me.

We do not find an explicit exploration of female ambivalence in *Chéri*, but we do in one of Colette's most celebrated short stories, which I shall now re-examine. It has haunted me ever since I first read it, precisely because it dares to raise the spectre of women's murderous feelings.

4

UNMOTHERED UNTETHERED

I chose to reread *La Lune de pluie* (1940) (*The Rainy Moon*) because I remembered how much it intrigued me on first reading. I was in my late thirties, having recently returned from living abroad part-time for several years, having left my marriage, being homeless and penniless, trying to scrape a living as a freelance. Blundering through this crisis, I felt plunged not only into the practical difficulties of the present but also into memories and images erupting from my unconscious mind, reframing questions about love and identity. The level of myth seemed just as relevant as that of the arguments of divorce lawyers. I ended up writing a play, *The Journeywoman* (1987),[1] about Psyche and her search for Eros, and that sustained me. Soul food. Literature in general was soul food. *La Lune de pluie* was inspiring not least because it reminded me that disorder and pain could spur creativity.

As a piece of art, *La Lune de pluie* seemed as complete in itself, as rounded and full, as the image at its core: the little 'rainbow halo' created on the inside wall of a Paris apartment by a bubble of coarse glass in the windowpane touched by sunlight. This apparently innocuous phenomenon, described near the start of the story, turns out to have wonderfully sinister implications.

Antonia White in her translation offers 'blister of glass' for *soufflure de verre*, but that metaphor hints at something negative, painful, too early on. I prefer 'bubble of glass', which is more accurate anyway, recalling *souffler* in its sense of glass-blowing. Almost immediately, it is true, Colette does seem to hint at mysterious happenings, when she deploys the term *apparition* for the rainy moon. However, that does not have to refer to ghosts, as it so often does in English; it can be translated simply as 'appearance'. This ambiguity of meaning suggests that the story is strolling rather than hurrying towards the uncanny. A few lines further on, we are indeed told that the rainy moon is viewed by a character in the story as a 'sad little sun', even as an 'omen'. Colette's first-person narrator resists this interpretation, suggesting it is one of the other woman's 'charming poetic fantasies'. To herself, though, she calls the rainy moon a *fantome*, a ghost. This defensiveness about naming, this slipperiness of reference, puts the reader on the alert. Words are unsteady, unreliable, and so the world they describe may be too. What is our narrator up to?

Rereading, I felt like a detective, snooping along sentence by sentence, collecting clues as to the story's meaning. These were sometimes unobtrusive, unremarkable, like bits of broken glass in a gutter. When struck by sunlight, however, these may turn to jewels. Yes, like rainy moons. I picked up what seemed to me keywords, key images, and made a mosaic with them; my own version of Colette's text. I discovered that the rainy moon does indeed focus the entire story. It introduces the idea of looking at ordinary things differently. 'Reality' may thereby be enhanced or distorted. A realist mode of writing (as I suggested in Chapter 1) may invoke the idea of narrative as a windowpane of plain, clear glass through which we survey the world outside. The language of the narrative becomes invisible; the world beyond seems objectively described. By contrast, the bubble of glass that is the rainy moon brings the outside inside, in the form of a rainbow inscribed on the wall. The image pushes the reader to notice the narrator's manipulation of language.

Technically, I suppose, a long short story, coming in at forty pages, *La Lune de pluie* could also count as a novella. However, it feels as satisfying, in its compression and intensity, as any of Colette's novels, in fact richer than quite a few of them. In those forty pages it covers haunting and the occult, sexual jealousy, memory, imagination, doubles, the uncanny, writing, storytelling, the unconscious, loss, hatred, murder, pleasure, the relationship between sisters, friendship, liminal states, and revenge.

The rainy moon itself is physically small, but it functions as a metaphor for something larger. It stands for and summons (as does the glass ball of the fairground clairvoyant) a strange world teeming with suggestion, ambiguous meanings. As a form of story, it is a coiled ball of images that unreels into a narrative propelled by the narrator's curiosity. Using the first person to tell the story, she does not name herself, but appears to be Colette. A younger version of the author. Also, the story reveals, a self haunted by her own ghost.

Right at the start we discover we are in the territory of the uncanny. Colette has arrived in a particular district of Montmartre, where she once lived, some time ago. She hardly recognizes it now, as buildings and even streets have changed, or vanished altogether. Visiting for the first time Rosita Berberet, the typist who will put her manuscript in order, she enters an ostensibly unfamiliar apartment, which Rosita shares with her younger sister Delia. Nonetheless Colette begins to sense she knows her way around it. Idly lifting the cheesecloth curtain veiling the window in the salon, glancing out into the street, she casually grasps the iron window catch. 'Immediately, I felt that slight vertigo, rather pleasant, which accompanies dreams of falling and of flying' (*LLP* 97; *TRM* 134). Her hand recognizes the form of the swivelling catch, shaped like a little mermaid, and then her brain affirms that indeed she remembers it.

The mermaid sounds the alert. Mermaids, as we know, are mythical creatures, half woman and half fish. In their current Disneyfied incarnation they seem to me to be sanitized, sentimentalized versions of their earlier selves; merely pretty and girly and unthreatening. However, when they surface in the legends, poetry, and paintings of the past, they carry troubling meanings, can evoke both fascination and fear. They are liminal creatures. Traditionally, they moved between and linked separated realms: land and sea, the world above water and the land below it. For some, they represent the conscious and unconscious layers of the psyche. In their malevolent aspect as feminine monsters they pretend to the human sexuality they lack (having no genitals) and seduce sailors to drown, having first bewitched them with their exquisite singing. Looked at in this way, they appear to be objects in a male story, props designed to carry and contain misogynistic fears about female sexuality, the power of cunts to draw men in, swallow them up. Men desiring beautiful women may lose control, may get dragged down into dangerous depths and die. This meaning is certainly hinted at in the denouement of Colette's tale. Looked at in another way, mermaids can be said to be allegorical figures, to represent symbols themselves: mermaids are half visible (above the waist/above the sea) and half invisible (below the waist/ below the sea), and symbols classically have one 'foot' in the visible, real world and one in the intangible, numinous one of dreams and spirituality.

Colette, laying her hand on the iron mermaid window catch, is laying claim to richly layered territory, and hinting at the hazards, mysteries, and terrors to come. Allowing physical touch to trigger memory, showing us how her hand 'knows' something before her brain does, she reveals a key aspect of her work: it embraces and reintegrates mind and body. In the Christian/bourgeois culture of her time they were conceptually separated (as I have already mentioned), mind (associated with men) valued more highly than body (associated with women), but the sensual intelligence of her writing links them, makes their interrelatedness a truth.

Bodily knowledge disrupts conventional linear notions of time. When, at Colette's touch, the past jumps up and confronts her, she understands that in fact she lived here, in this apartment, many years previously. She has tried to forget that episode, for her own good reasons, but without complete success. Currently the walls are almost entirely covered with 'gloomy steel engravings framed in black' and 'coloured reproductions of prints' but 'a few square inches of wallpaper remained bare' and on them Colette spots the faded pattern she once knew well, 'in short, the shadow [ombre] of a bunch of flowers repeated a hundred times' (LLP 97; TRM 134). For ombre Antonia White gives 'ghost', but Colette's term is subtler, less spelt out. She leaves it to us to work out that the patch of faded wallpaper on the walls cluttered with pictures may be an image of the past obscured by the present; an image of vain attempts utterly to forget. Three pages further on, Colette compares herself to Proust. He pursued a 'bygone and completed time'. Colette suggests that, by contrast, her own past is constantly revealing itself, often when she least expects it, and she names it significantly as a mermaid raising its dripping head as it rises from the depths.

The opening of the story establishes writing as a key theme. Colette and Rosita Barberet establish their working arrangement: on each visit Colette will collect the previous batch of material and hand over a new one to be typed. The work in question is fiction. Colette, having been commissioned by a big daily paper to produce a serial suitable for its mass readership, has been having trouble writing it, producing only clumsy first drafts of early episodes. At the same time she hints that the story of her own life, if she tries to tell it, is hardly a seamless, elegantly flowing narrative. The reader infers that Colette has had several goes, in fits and starts, at living well, not just at writing well. Through visiting an apartment, one of whose inhabitants, Delia, is revealed as trapped inside a self-spun web of fantasy to do with sexual desire and lust for revenge, Colette is pushed to remember her own experience of break-ups and abandonment. Her memories move in and out of the foreground, as the story proceeds. The structure of *La Lune de pluie* is complex, cunning, and delicately wrought, though we may not see that on a first reading. I certainly did not. I just gulped the story down—a cocktail of nectar with a touch of bitters—and did not analyse its form. Colette was my writing mentor: I was enchanted by her tale of a writer acknowledging personal pain and difficulty and summoning curiosity in order to deal with them, and willingly followed her tale wherever it led me. Colette was my Eve: she pursued experience, she wanted to gain sensual wisdom, she was willing to take risks.

Colette appears to be writing about loss, and the emptiness at the heart of a rejected woman's life, but at exactly the same time she gives us a vision of fullness. Reflecting on how the lulls between love affairs with men can be soothing and healing, she recalls how (as I mention/discuss in Chapter 2) she has previously likened those periods to the blank pages that separate the chapters of a book. In *La Lune de pluie* she reminds us that printers call these pages 'beautiful pages', and she precisely links them with 'beautiful days' spent working, street-sauntering, enjoying the company of friends, episodes she recounts with lightness, a touch of humour.

As *la Lune de pluie* demonstrates, the apparently empty pages may contain the most thrilling and disturbing episodes in a woman's life. In this particular evocation of the white spaces, Colette may be refining her earlier definition, may be implicitly suggesting that affairs with men structure a woman's experience strictly and narrowly, according to the man-made rules of the culture, whereas periods without men offer freedom: the woman has to invent and live her own story. However, these independently created narratives may prove unacceptable, since they do not fit into the formal and moral structures of standard novels, or standard magazine serials: they may be too experimental, or, as in Delia's case, involve perversion and 'nameless filth'. I read them as written in Colette's particular version of invisible ink, pale perhaps but definitely there, like the lemon juice I experimented with as a child playing at being a spy and writing in code. For example, avoiding the cliché that only adventures with men are worth exploring in fiction, Colette hints at the delights and freedoms of female friendship, invoking long bike rides with her dear friend Annie de Pêne. She gives us just a glimpse of these pleasures, in a couple of sentences. Similarly, with regard to Delia's schemes, she invites us to decipher what she means by her shorthand 'nameless filth'. Colette, it seems to me, provokes the reader to squint at the possible meaning of such a term. Colette herself is laying the paper trail, throwing out tantalizing clues (her characters' gestures, silences, actions) as to Delia's fragmented and changing story, and to her own, which possibly mirrors it in certain ways. Is this a love story? A murder mystery? A horror story? Colette refuses to name it, which could mean defusing its power. She simply draws our attention not only to the mermaid catch but also to the rainy moon that apparently frightens Delia, to Delia's attraction to needles and sharp-pointed scissors, and to Delia's confession that she is planning something in her head that's 'a bit like a novel, only better'.

Colette is affronted by this competitiveness, not least because she has been having trouble with her own writing. She has protested to her editor 'in all honesty' that she has no idea how to produce the serial novel he wants. That sounds modest. Perhaps there is some anger or self-disgust involved: perhaps the commission involves betraying her talent, churning out superficial, false copy. Colette does not say. In any case, she prepares to abandon her attempt after just a few tries. She decides to turn this 'failure' to good account, to choose a form that better suits her: to write short stories. *La Lune de pluie* may be one of them. In exemplary modernist fashion, it declares its origins, its conditions of making. We witness its author, and her avatar, struggling to tell it, to give it a shape, and having trouble doing so. She imagines giving one version of it to her beloved Annie, who will shrug at it; she recounts giving another version of it to her laundress/friend Marie, who urges her on. She invites us to become questioning readers. Is she caught inside the story or is she in control of it? Is she a collaborator in Delia's story-inside-the-story or is she the heroine of her own tale? Is she an innocent searcher after truth or is she a nosy parker? At different moments she is all of these.

La Lune de pluie also confronts us with questions of literary judgement. What makes a good story? In this case it seems to involve apparent emotional truthfulness and precision contrasting with playfulness and teasing, narrative sophistication masquerading as simplicity, and well-controlled dramatic timing and tension.

I am struck by how seductive Colette is in this story. She herself is feeling seduced by beautiful, sulky, secretive Delia, by the mystery inside the flat, unable to resist returning to it, trying to ferret out what is going on, and she constantly invites us to collude with her. She draws us in with her wry humour, her frank disclosures, her intimate revelations, as though she is a friend gossiping beside us on the sofa.

Confession? Flirtation? Her narration seems artless and sincere. However, she manipulates our responses with great skill. First of all she makes us feel safe. Welcomed. Yes, do come in, my dears. Then she begins subtly to make us doubt our grip on reality. She unobtrusively introduces a different kind of reality, the invisible layered onto the visible, somehow glimmering behind it, through it. What-is-there merges with what-is-not-there. The resultant what-is-there is definitely spooky. A doorbell, that ordinary, banal feature of domestic life, serves this purpose. Immediately after her first visit to the Barberet sisters, Colette describes a fantasy of climbing the stairs in an apartment block, arriving on a certain floor, and ringing a doorbell, then, in a violent switch of perspective, opening her flat door to her younger double. On her second visit to the Barberets, she notices the modern electric bellpush at the entrance to the apartment, which replaces the pearl-beaded strip of braid for tugging the manually worked bell that she installed years back. She can 'see' this. A displaced, remembered feature of decor has no reason to scare us, but the suggestion is that strange presences are hovering beyond the appearances of material objects and want to behave not like well-brought-up visitors, politely ringing a doorbell, but interlopers determined to slither in, possess us, hurt us. It is hardly coincidental that Colette presents us with an image of liminality so close to the start of the story. She is flagging up that we are on the threshold of a different, potentially threatening world. (Later, Colette encounters Delia, in an apparent swoon, actually lying on the floor just behind the front door of the flat.) Of course, as a writer, a storyteller, Colette knows that this is precisely her mermaid job: to lure us somewhere new, to employ imagination to create, alter, and disrupt entire worlds. She is a magician, transforming what may be rooted in autobiography into a tale shimmering with potential horror. Inside an ordinary apartment in Montmartre she summons the uncanny. Certainties and fixed meanings flicker and dissolve. Metaphors dance like ghouls.

Rereading this story was certainly beguiling, but I am finding it difficult to write about it. My thoughts blunder and falter. Words are greased wrestlers, tripping me up, slipping away. Writing about La Lune de pluie I keep stopping. Floored. Is that because the story is so powerful, so complete, that it silences me? It frightens me? I want to leave it behind, feel that it is definitely finished and over, rather than dive back into it? I will try and articulate the problems, and see where that takes me.

For a start (as I commented above in Chapter 2, concerning novels) it is difficult to say what a story is about. You have got to enter it, participate in it, witness it. If I try to tell you the story of this story, I am in danger of getting caught up in that joky Borgesian dilemma: making an exact copy, repeating Colette word for word. However, as soon as I tell myself that it is impossible to summarize *La Lune de pluie*, to recount its plot, I have to recognize that in fact it is, crucially, all about plotting. Delia is planning to wreak revenge on her estranged husband, and Colette gradually finds this out once she has opened a well-remembered door beside the fireplace in the salon and pushed her way into the back room of the flat (or we could say opened a door in her mind and pushed her way into its further recesses). Here she encounters the strange and disturbed younger sister. Subsequently she coaxes the reluctant older sister to explain a little of what may be going on. Gradually revealing to the reader the extent to which she can identify with an abandoned young woman languishing after a lost love, at the same time Colette cannot bear to imagine that she could once have been fired by similar rage. She deploys a light tone, insists that she suffered her own break-up 'without bitterness'. My own break-up? I remember mainly the relief at having escaped, and my exhaustion after the effort involved. My thirst for revenge surfaced only years later and spent itself enjoyably in the writing of an episode, a comic pastiche of De Sade, in my novel *Flesh and Blood* (1994). Delia's plot to make her husband suffer fires the plot of *La Lune de pluie*. Colette's valiant struggles as a young woman to overcome her own suffering float along as a disturbing subtext, another current of emotion and meaning.

It is also difficult to discuss this story precisely because of its layered form, its layered effects, present and past coexisting in a kind of magical linguistic millefeuille, even though, of course, it is a narrative existing in sentence-by-sentence time, one thing happening after another, one thing leading to and conjuring another. It functions as a metaphor-based poem does, through a structure of connected imagery. This form, rounded and compressed as the rainy moon of the title, leaps free under the reader's sunbeam gaze, sending colours swinging in all directions. Aha. Now that I describe the story as working like a poem, I see that in fact it works like a specific, particular sort of versification: a spell. If this story–spell bewitches, entrances, and frightens me, no wonder. Delia is casting a spell with evil intentions. At the same time, Colette is casting a spell over me, drawing me into a complex web of images whose hallucinatory, multifaceted intensity arrests me. I am held spellbound. In this sense, Colette is not only a sweet-voiced mermaid enticing me into the delightful world of imagination but also a dangerous one, gripping me and not letting me go. I am the entrapped sailor. Colette's writing summons forces and energies that threaten to overwhelm me.

Part of my bewitchment and difficulty involves being drawn into the complicated time scheme of the story. It plays with, crucially pivots around, different, coexisting layers of time. There is the present of the narrative happening on the page as I read it greedily in the here and now, when everything about it seems new, happening for the first time, even on a rereading. There is the present tense that Colette the author inhabits when she poses rhetorical questions to her reader, or when she addresses us directly: 'the allure of the past is more forceful than the thirst for knowing the future … a shock … I cannot lucidly describe … Just imagine' (*LLP* 101; *TRM* 138). Then there is the past. The main events of the story are narrated in the past tense, and concern the fairly distant past, when Colette makes the first of her several visits to the Berberet sisters' apartment. Over weeks and months, from late winter to summer, the mystery deepens and unfolds. Colette is also recounting events and moods recurring to her memory that happened in the more distant past, concerning her youthful struggles to write and live well. *La Lune de pluie* confronts the reader with muddled, confused, and confusing time. While revealing how the past constantly interrupts and infuses the present, it also enacts that. No wonder I feel lost and fear drowning as I plunge down through these layers of narrative.

I have another, connected, reason to feel disturbed by this story. Its embodiment of layers of memory reminds me of fugue states I have experienced in the past and also hints at their possible return. What is a fugue state? For me, an explosion of memory, a flood of memory coexisting with a temporary loss of awareness about the immediate past/the present, where I am, who I am. Why does one happen? As I have experienced fugue (is that even the right word? I don't know), it is brought on by different triggers.

Some seem purely visual. For example, I have unwittingly hypnotized myself by becoming entranced by candlelight glittering on the foam of a bath taken lengthily in a darkened bathroom, and also by sunlight dancing on waves as I swam happily and mindlessly up and down in a summer sea. On those occasions I got lost in a dazzling array of prelinguistic images. If I was meeting my mermaid self, in her watery habitat, I did not enjoy the encounter.

Another trigger is language. For example, a few years ago, returning to a volume of Renaissance love poetry I had not opened since I was 18, I not only re-encountered my earlier self but became her, remembered exactly what I was thinking and feeling when I first read those poems by Donne, Drayton, Marvell. There I newly was, ardent, naive, enraptured, shivering in my freezing college room with its view over the dustbins and at the same time dwelling in the presence of the poets, hearing them speak to me across centuries, dissolve time and space. The poems had acted as a mnemonic, very powerfully so. Feelings had soaked into the language printed on the page and returned to me as I reread it. In one way that was pleasurable. In another way it was frightening, because I did not know how to get back to me-in-the-present. I suppose that in the end I just shut the book.

The third kind of trigger for jolting me into a fugue state is unacknowledged internal conflict; just too much going on. When I was younger, this happened in the aftermath of a passionate affair with a married man, all to do with desire and guilt and anger, a mix I could not contain, made more difficult by connecting me to the sexy feelings I had as a young girl about my father, my muddle about whether fantasy was in fact literal truth, my unarticulated sense that I was irredeemably wicked. Incest was so taboo that I could not let myself know I was desiring it. I mentioned above, in Chapter 1, my sense of being a family outcast. My fear of incest deepened that sense. In my memoir *Paper Houses* (2007) I wrote about going into therapy, certain I needed it but not knowing why. I could not even name the problem, and nor could the therapist. When I revealed my discomfort about older, married men chatting me up, she made me feel I was merely priggish. A mutual friend told me years later that this woman had had 'a love affair' with her own father. She admitted at the end of the therapy that we had never sorted out my 'sexual problem'. Perhaps the therapeutic problem was also on her side. However, the 'failure' of that aspect of the therapy (which helped me a lot in other ways) opened up possibilities for change. Beginning to write short stories, and then a novel, gave me a way through, showing me that I could trust my imagination as a creative force, even if the things I imagined sometimes scared me.

However it is provoked, the fugue entails drifting into a timeless space where every single moment I have lived is present, a pattern in constant movement, where the whole of memory surrounds my lost 'I' in the form of twinkling images, a kind of mad abstract, a mad mandala, beautiful but also frightening. I described a fugue state in *Negative Capability* (2020), as indeed falling into it became the reason for beginning to write the book, to try and reconnect the bits of my shattered, scattered self. I ended up with a memoir; a representation of temporarily achieved coherence. There was no story; just diary accounts of particular days across a year. I had put my shattered self back into narrative time. Crucially (obviously) doing that involved deploying language; finding one word to go after another. Emerging from speechlessness.

That links to what I wrote about in Chapter 3: Chéri leaves his timeless prelapsarian world and becomes born into language. A writer does this, over and over again, each time she begins writing a novel. She moves horizontally from the entrancing inner world whirling with visual images and enters the outer world, where language waits, and she moves vertically from the unconscious to the conscious. Her writing self wanders back and forth between these different worlds, both up and down and also across from one to another. She is a flâneuse, idling along boulevards of language. When the writing is going well, the writer forgets herself completely and merges with the flow of words. A kind of fugue state, yes, but one that is less frightening than welcome, because it is dynamically linked to making something; it involves a relationship with material.

The compression of and play with time characterizing *La Lune de pluie*, its sparkling array of images, do remind me of fugue states. I think that Colette is writing about something similarly intensely felt. She is describing being haunted by her younger self and by the rush of emotion that brings with it. At first, near the start of the story, she describes the possibly dangerous allure of the past, the ambiguous attraction of revisiting old 'haunts', how (as I mention above) she can dream of opening her flat door to her younger self: 'The end is missing. But as good nightmares go, it's a beauty' (*LLP* 103; *TRM* 139). Further in, she wonders what she can have bequeathed to the rainy moon to have changed it into an emblem of something evil that the unstable, intuitive Delia has picked up. Next, we realize that, when she recognizes Delia as a possible version of herself, she is admitting that she too could have harboured disturbing wishes. Her memory of her own unhappiness rises up and meshes with Delia's. Colette has wanted to think she has left that wretched younger self behind, like a dead person, a dead body, but it resurrects itself, comes rushing up, alive and menacing, to disturb her. She dreams that she actually is Delia.

Colette takes the trope of the haunted house and makes it modern. No gothic cellars and attics: this is a haunted apartment, up to date, given banal contemporary features such as the onyx-style glass bowl of the ceiling light, the picture frames of plaited straw. The haunting is unexpected precisely because the setting is so ordinary, so contemporary. I do not expect a ghost to appear in this kind of genteel interior jumbled with cane tables and tubular umbrella stands.

Ghost stories can scare and disturb me partly because they mix up past, present, and future. They unsettle any narrative I want to believe in that flows smoothly along like conventional biography from life to death. The classic sort of ghost returns from a place beyond death, the future to which we are all heading, and appears to me in the present, and makes me see and think about the past, when the ghost was a flesh-and-blood live being. We deal with our confusion about these time-disrupting visions by narrating them, putting them into stories told in the past tense. Ghost stories are necessarily retrospective. Ghosts may appear to a person as a visual image but to be shown to others need to be translated into language, embedded in narrative. You re-create the ghost by telling a story about it. In fact, a ghost may be recognized as such only by having a tale subsequent to its sighting recounted. A ghost could be understood, as I suggest in my essay 'A Many-Storied House' (2021)² as a story demanding to be told. In *La Lune de pluie* Colette presents Delia as like a ghost spotted in traditional shiver-inducing tales of the supernatural, lurking in shadowy corners, lying in wait unseen behind doors, emanating threat. Colette, the ghost-hunter, will discover and tell her story.

At the same time, another ghost shimmers in the darkness behind Delia; another story nudges up behind hers, demands to be told. We glimpse the repressed story that Colette wants to ignore but feels forced to face: that story of her own abandonment, loss, loneliness, abjection. Where one of Delia's occult practices consists of a kind of perverse praying, the constant reiteration of her lost husband's name to *convoquer* ('summon') supremely malevolent forces and energies that will punish him, Colette calls up benevolent energies and creative forces. She lays her own ghost by weaving it into a story. At its end, you get a strong sense of her making a knot, biting off the end of her thread, pushing the work away. There. It is finished. Completed. The past is done with. For the moment, anyway.

La Lune de pluie offers a suggestive and ambiguous depiction of Delia and Colette mastering tricky circumstances in their own different ways, and this consoled me as a younger woman dealing with the loss of home and of security. It inspires me now, reminding me, when I feel overwhelmed by life's difficulties, that I am strong enough to get up and act and find solutions, or, at least, to act as though that were the case.[3]

La Lune de pluie reminds me of how closely creativity in art is linked to destruction. When we begin writing, we may admire and copy old models, and learn a lot that way. Then we find that we want to destroy old patterns of words, then play and experiment with the fragments, put them together differently, create new patterns, make new narratives. I used to imagine I was working with shards of a broken pot I had discovered, never seen whole. (I did not specify/admit that I myself might have smashed the pot. Why not? Fear of recognizing my own aggression, I suppose.) When I made something new, I was working with gaps, chipped bits. I left the joins showing. (A while back I discovered this is close to a Japanese technique in mending pottery, in which the joins may be painted gold.) Something similar can happen in life, as I described in *Negative Capability*. Art and life fused: writing a book about crisis and feeling broken, I simultaneously recomposed a self, a tentative sense of identity; one with the cracks showing.

La Lune de pluie separates out the urges to create and to destroy. In the end, Colette-the-narrator acts creatively, composing the story and also leaving the Berberet sisters behind, while Delia acts destructively, composing her spell and leaving her husband behind. (I shall not spell out precisely what happens at the end of the story, since I hope you will find out for yourselves. Colette, in any case, offers us merely a telling visual image.) Colette chooses a positive solution and Delia a negative one. There is a hint, though, that Colette, despite recoiling from Delia, will necessarily remember their similarity, their connection.

The entire story could indeed be viewed as a collaged picture of an unhappy self struggling to survive. If we cannot cope with internal conflict, say between desire and rage, or if we cannot cope with ambivalence, cannot cope with how love and hate dance back to back, or if we cannot bear to acknowledge that what we do clashes with what we would like to think about ourselves, we may dissociate. We may split ourselves in two. The story suggests this to me through its deployment of significant pairings, of doubles. The double is, of course, a well- known trope in gothic and horror fiction, introducing speculation on repressed memory, repressed desire. Colette offers us a series of mirrorings, which act powerfully to destabilize any humanist notion we may want to cherish of secure, centred identity, any realist literary notion of single well-rounded character. She encourages us to question the meaning of terms such as reality and reflected reality, reality and illusion, literal and metaphorical. Some of these binaries, these differences, seem invoked in order to make us question how and why they are given moral value according to the rules of language. Real and unreal. Stable and unstable. Conscious and unconscious. In terms of personae, of aspects of character, some of the pairs are presented as equal couples, each as important as the other. For example, we encounter Colette-the-writer and Colette-the-narrator, as I have indicated throughout. (Though I could also state that one contains the other.) Some pairs have the uncertain power relationships of siblings: Colette-the-narrator confronts Colette-her-younger-self. Yet other pairings confront us with the hierarchical values placed by our culture on certain differences. Colette the writer of books nervously faces Rosita the secretary, the typer of books. Rosita, the 'withered' (as Antonia White puts it) young–old spinster, is despised by her ardent, sexually experienced younger sister, Delia. Rosita is healthy and Delia is ill. Colette recognizes Delia as her shadow, her potential 'bad' self. Yet more pairings indicate mutual generosity. Colette, busily inventing dramas, is checked by her realistic and practical friend Annie de Pêne. Colette the daughter, maker of stories, faces her mother, Sido, the maker of children, the adored encourager of her talent.

Sido's abrupt, unexpected entrance into the story, towards its end, signals the possibility of the renewal of life, balance, and sanity. She stands for an organizing principle of psychic health, since she is the keeper of the past, and of childhood, while also insisting on the importance of living in and cherishing the present. It is as though she introduces time into the whirling dance of personages in the eternal now of the unconscious. In *La Lune de pluie* she stands precisely, not for the idealized mother of *La Maison de Claudine*, not for the incestuous mother of Chéri's fantasy of prelapsarian, wordless union, but for the earthy goddess who can name all the birds and beasts and plants in her warm, domestic, local paradise. She brings Colette a weathervane in the shape of a nosegay of oats (stitched onto cardboard, they droop at the approach of rain). Ripe oats signify summer and fruition and harvest. Handing them to Colette–Persephone, Demeter–Sido is reminding her to live inside time, to recognize the turning of seasons from winter to spring, the possibility of moving away from lingering in sickness back towards developing health. Sido's message, I now realize, looking back, certainly worked for me when I was younger. It has only strengthened with the years. Whenever I am floundering in difficulties, my Demeter-friends remind me: this hard time will end, you will get through this, as you have done before.

Delia prefers to live solely in her own deranged imagination. Colette, as the protagonist of her own tale, knows how to inhabit a world of sensual pleasure and let it nourish her. For her this often means gourmandize. Arriving in Montmarte at the opening of the story, she joyously re-encounters the sweet shop of old: 'Pink sugared almonds in bowls, redcurrant balls in brimming glass jars, emerald-coloured mints and beige caramels' (*LLP* 101; *TRM* 137). She invokes picnics shared with Annie de Pêne: 'We would take our bicycles, a fresh loaf stuffed with butter and sardines, two puff-pastry sausage rolls, bought at a delicatessen near la Muette, and some apples, the whole fastened with string to a wicker-jacketed bottle full of white wine' (*LLP* 106; *TRM* 141). She remembers the market in the Rue des Martyrs, with its shops displaying chickens, legs of mutton, sausages, chicory, fruit, and dates. This capacity to translate her love of food into sensual images implies her sanity, signals how she can take care of herself properly, give herself pleasure, feed her imagination with a wide range of stimuli. When she brings the Berberet sisters a gift of ripe cherries, she recognizes that Delia may allow herself to enjoy eating them but cannot sustain an interest in them for long. Delia relapses, her preferred 'food' her gorging on corrupted desire.

What stays with me most strongly from this reading of *The Rainy Moon* is Colette's description of that market: 'I admired the oranges between the open sacks of rice and the sweating coffee, the red apples and the green split peas. Just as in Nice one covets the entire flower market with its massed flowers, so here I would have bought a whole stall of foodstuffs, from the early lettuces to the blue packets of semolina' (*LLP* 118; *TRM* 151). She wants everything. The life force courses through her. We know she will survive.

I am particularly moved by Colette's acknowledgement of wanting everything, because as a Catholic I was brought up to believe that wanting and desiring, particularly for women, who were instructed to be self-denying and wholly focussed on helping others, were sinful. Repression was preached as the aim. Hunger for food and love could easily turn into greed and lust. Aggression was dangerously unfeminine. Colette's biography reveals her scorn for such prohibitions. She celebrated her robust, healthy body, took many lovers, displayed herself half-naked as a mime on stage, ate and drank with gusto, allowed herself to become large, accepted the aggression involved in the drive to write and to perfect writing. She loved herself, approved of her own desires. She had found her creative power, and it was linked to appetite.

If we start off in infancy by exploring the world through our mouths, through our hunger linked to our curiosity and to our desires for pleasure and satisfaction, Colette shows us that, as adults, we can cherish these energies rather than feel obliged to repudiate them; we can link them to our need to explore the world in thought, through creativity. She expresses that through describing, in the heart of her story, that Montmartre market brimming with delights. No need to eat everything in sight, as the baby might try to do (or as the baby-in-me might want to do when in the throes of hopeless need): she can possess the foods and fruits through translating them into joyfully sensual language. Her imagery is not decorative, not merely descriptive, but fundamental to her vision. The literal and the metaphorical seem to fuse. The gorgeous fruits of the earth perish, and also they remain, ripened and sweet, in memory and imagination, and in Colette's words.

CONCLUSION

Rereading these four works by Colette has only deepened my admiration of her writing and my gratitude for what writing that has taught me.

A memoir. Two novels. A novella. In each of them Colette displays radical originality. She reinvents the form each time, as I have tried to show, mixing elements of different sorts of texts. She ignores conventional notions about storytelling, balance, and coherence. For example, in *La Lune de pluie* she mentions Marie her laundress/friend in one breath and dispatches her in the next; she introduces Annie de Pêne with no explanation; she abruptly brings Sido on stage right at the end. She is a pioneer of what we now call autofiction: she draws upon what are apparently moments of raw personal experience—delving into subjects such as childhood, desire, ageing, loss—and transforms these into subtle, suggestive, satisfying works of art, into narratives embodying stories that are also open-ended meditations. The works operate on various levels. We are shown the external world, in its material, sensually perceived reality, mapped onto the internal world of thought, dream, memory, vision. The two mesh, providing and enriching ways of seeing and understanding. We are led into myths, and out again. We are invited to notice the writer's doubts, hesitations about what she is up to, as well as her delight in nailing particular perceptions.

Colette conceals her writerly sophistication, thereby giving us the pleasure of discovering it. For example: I found myself nudged, rather than instructed, to notice the way in which the gaps and white spaces in her text can operate as peepholes into other possible stories. Colette invites us to become active collaborators in working out what may be going on when words suddenly stop. She invites us to become active readers. She calls to us to come and play.

I think of writing as a form of play. I am a kid messing about in the sandpit, happily making soft sculptures then happily destroying them then starting again. Later on, my adult self arrives on the scene to help with editing, revising, redrafting. When I was younger, she was often a punitive figure, telling me my work was rubbish. I turned her into a caricature, Mother Superior bashing me with her rolling pin, but now, thanks to my reading and rereading Colette, I am constantly reminded that, just as child (Colette) and mother (Sido) can engage happily with each other, so too can the writing self and the editing self. That image of inner cooperation links to my memory of how my mother and I learned to forgive each other, redefine loving each other. Now, when my writing self quarrels with my editing self, I know I have got to stay with the conflict, give difficulties time to settle, trust that I will be able to sort things out. In the real world of publishing, I can re-experience this conflict, wanting to turn in wildly experimental books, or books full of everything I am thinking, rather than listen to an editor counselling restraint. If the editor sounds too brisk, it is still easy to project the controlling Mother Superior figure of childhood onto her, to want to rebel against her, stamp my foot and have a tantrum. I am disconcerted by that cross toddler jumping up inside me. Yet I know she gives me energy; she demands to be heard; she may be offering new ideas on how to play.

Having felt tugged to reread these four books of Colette's that circle around or invoke the mother–child relationship, I have clarified for myself that Sido was indeed Colette's muse, introducing her to a distinctive earthly paradise combining the natural world and the library. The original paradise, the dream (the fantasized memory) of union with the mother, has necessarily to be lost and mourned. Then it can be regained in an altered form, through being reinvented in play, in imagination, in love. Sido created her world (bedroom to kitchen to street) by interacting with it and naming it, and taught her daughter to do likewise. Paradise Regained becomes less a place than a way of being: living in the present, cherishing the ordinary, the everyday, valuing friendship, relishing all sorts of pleasure while not fleeing suffering, trying to understand feeling. These are energies emphasized throughout Colette's work, with its delight in sensual experience, its assertion that humans are kin to animals, its linking of feeling and thought, its willingness to examine pain. For this exploration language is necessary. The reward for leaving the original paradise, or the dream of paradise, and its shadow, the dream of incest, is entering language, as we saw in my chapter on *Chéri*.

Sido is presented as someone who talks to her daughter. Colette talks back. She recomposes her mother's life in writing: as stories, as vignettes, as visions, as hallucinations, as overheard speech. She demonstrates Sido inviting her to the mother–daughter dancing game of attachment and loss, of leaving and returning. Colette's developed genius enables her to write brilliantly about having, and not having, about leaving a home and finding a home. Many of my novels feature young women leaving home and starting out on quests, examining what the notion of home may mean. Rereading Colette, I stop worrying that this is too well worn a theme and simply see I have found one of my main subjects. The young woman inside me still feels clamorously alive. She often feels more real to me than the fact that I am ageing. When I remember how old I am, it is a shock. Inside I feel 35. I still want to leave home and have adventures. I have not let go of that wish.

Colette writes decisively about letting go. An important theme in these four works, this is presented as a major, necessary component of ageing. Colette suggests that letting go of sexual desire, the past, hurts, and grudges, is freeing. Letting go of beloved people and places paradoxically enables their re-creation in art, and so their repossession, in a new form. Letting go brings its own reward. It all seems wonderfully positive.

When I look again, I feel more ambivalent. Colette's playing a game, isn't she? That is certainly the case in La Naissance du jour. All the time she is preaching renunciation, showing us how to accept ageing and being alone, she is frolicking with a husband fifteen years younger than she is. Frolicking carefully. She and Maurice maintained separate bedrooms, and Colette received him in the mornings only once she was fully made up and groomed.[1]

Colette's gift to me, in this respect, therefore, is not mealy-mouthed clichés about patience and resignation but stringent advice for both writing and life: accept ambivalence, be contradictory if necessary, play tricks when you want to. Invent for yourself how you deal with ageing. Other people's versions may not suit.

Sido's generosity towards her daughter crucially involved the gift of thinking freely. Colette became an amoral writer, one who quickly shed the narrow-minded Catholicism of her village background and who seems unmarked by it. Armed with

Sido's willingness to reassess conventional distinctions between sin and virtue, Colette developed inner strength, a lack of guilt, an unashamed curiosity. She could bend a steady eye on the different worlds through which she moved, on the complicated ways in which men and women negotiated the power imbalances structuring their relationships. She recognized how class structured subjective experience. She surveyed and was (some of the time but not always) part of a world in which privileged women squeezed themselves into corsets of mind and body and (apparently) enjoyed being 'held' and dandled and controlled, and able to control servants and children, while other less privileged women, wise-cracking gallantly, matter-of-factly sold themselves in order to survive; a world in which women were routinely beaten up by jealous lovers and supposed to accept it as proof of male love; she looked at the tango between marriage and adultery, at the female competitiveness and spite that sexual inequality produced.

Now I can admire her willingness to keep looking, to get close up, to accept the flaws of her culture in order to describe them. However, as a young woman reading her for the first time, I sometimes felt distressed by her honesty. I admired what seemed her willingness to accept contradictions—for example, to flout feminine convention in some ways and yet to write about it semi-admiringly, affectionately, even with fascination. However, as a young feminist furious about misogyny and injustice, I wanted to be single-minded and heroic, to believe that women could change the world, change ourselves, change ways of living and loving. I was romantic and idealistic, and judged myself harshly whenever I fell short of my own high standards, which happened often. I took a while to realize that I was living feminism as though it were another form of church. I discovered, as soon as I began writing about female subjectivity, that I was writing not about heroines halfway to becoming perfected, like Catholic saints, but about women-as-heretics struggling to release and articulate unconscious thoughts and feelings, to explore taboos and clichés about femininity rather than simply reject them. If I felt trapped, I had to examine and describe the trap while I was trying to break out of it, just as Colette had done.

Imagination proved to be the key: a sort of knowing; a way of seeing. Using imagination produced, in Catholic terms, a sort of Transfiguration. Colette would not have employed that religious term, but her writing did begin to reveal to me a kind of bodily mysticism, a way of rejoicing in the radiant body of the world, a way of letting all one's hungers, however apparently childish or perverse, lead one there. Her writing pushed me on my heretic's quest to reintegrate body and soul (pompous as that sounds), in life and in novels and poems, helped me discover that the numinous was at the same time blissfully earthy, connected to physical memory, physical knowledge, physical desire. I ended up believing that artists help create the numinous, that their creativity cooperates with it, reveals it, by embodying it, giving it meaning. I demonstrated that in my novel *Cut Out* (2021) and I do not think I could have written that novel without Colette's inspiration.

So 'God' is a dead word, an absent word, and into that space floods art and poetry and novels. I do not think Colette bothered for a moment about God. She leapfrogged the struggle I had to get through the thickets of Catholic morality and misogyny. She simply learned from Sido to value this 'fallen', beautiful world that is so fragile and in such danger. Colette's capacity to love the earth and all its creatures links to current thinking about ecology. At the same time, though she loved creatures, she loved eating them too. In that respect she echoed the peasants of her village. You had one pig, you cared for it, then you killed it, and its meat lasted you and your family for a year. That unsentimentality characterizes Colette's thought.

Rereading Colette, I find my way back to my mother, to that unsentimental, strong, practical French woman who taught French language and literature, who gave me a French soul, who never gave up on me, even when she found my behaviour most baffling and hurtful.

Rereading Colette, I salute her freedom from guilt and shame, her amorality, her openness to new experiences, new thoughts, her cherishing of the subjects that approach her, her close examination of them: these qualities of hers inspire me to read better; to try to write better.

ACKNOWLEDGEMENTS

Thanks to Marina Warner, who suggested I write this book, to the series editor Philip Davis for his kindness, encouragement, and help with the index, to my agent, Charles Walker, for his expertise, wisdom, and humour, and to all at OUP for seeing things through. Thanks to the friends who variously talked to me about Colette's work, lent me books by her, read early drafts of my text, and generally encouraged me: Carmen Callil, Nell Dunn, Marguerite Defriez, Isobel Durrant, Hermione Lee, Sarah LeFanu, Jane Martineau, Cécile Menon, Ruthie Petrie, Helen Simpson, Wendy Vaizey, and Helen Walton.

NOTES

Introduction

1. Elaine Marks and Isabelle de Courtivron (eds), *New French Feminisms* (New York: Harvester Press, 1986).

Chapter 1

1. Quoted by Claude Pichois, 'Preface', in *LNJ*, 7.
2. Colette, 'Le Patriarche', in *Bella-Vista* (Paris: J. Ferenczi et fils, 1937); 'The Patriarch', in *TRM*.
3. Alain Brunet, 'Introduction', in *SVV*.
4. Margaret Crosland, *Madame Colette: A Provincial in Paris* (London: Peter Owen, 1954), 11.
5. Janice Radway, *Reading the Romance: Women, Patriarchy and Popular Literature* (London: Verso, 1987).
6. Marion Milner, *A Life of One's Own* (London: Routledge, 2011). (Thanks to Philip Davis, editor of this series, for pointing me in this direction.)
7. Raymond Mortimer, 'Introduction', in *CFC*.

Chapter 2

1. Colette, *Bella-Vista* (Paris: J. Ferenczi et fils, 1937); trans. Antonia White, in *The Rainy Moon and Other Stories* (Harmondsworth: Penguin, 1976).

Chapter 3

1. Colette, *Cheri* and *La Fin de Cheri*, trans. Roger Senhouse (Harmondsworth: Penguin Modern Classics, 1962) (*CFC*).
2. *TLS* 6220, 17 June 2022.

Chapter 4

1. Performed at the Mercury Theatre, Colchester, in 1987. Not published. Typescript.
2. Michèle Roberts, 'A Many-Storied House', in D. Coxon and R. V. Hirst (eds), *Writing the Uncanny: Essays on Crafting Strange Fiction* (London: Dead Ink/Cinder House Publishing, 2021), 25.
3. Thanks to Philip Davis for his insights on William James in his book *William James* (*My Reading* series; Oxford: Oxford University Press, 2022), *passim*.

Conclusion

1. Maurice Goudeket, *Close to Colette*, trans. Enid McLeod (London: Secker & Warburg, 1957).

SELECT BIBLIOGRAPHY

Works by Colette

Bella-Vista (Paris: J. Ferenczi et fils, 1937); in *The Rainy Moon and Other Stories*, trans. Antonia White (Harmondsworth: Penguin, 1976) (*TRM*).

Chéri (Paris: Livre de Poche, Fayard, 2021) (*Ch.*).

Chéri and *La Fin de Chéri*, trans. Roger Senhouse (Harmondsworth: Penguin Modern Classics, 1962) (*CFC*).

La Lune de pluie, in *Chambre d'hôtel suivi de La Lune de pluie* (Paris: Livre de Poche, Fayard, 1954) (*LLP*); in *The Rainy Moon and Other Stories*, trans. Antonia White (Harmondsworth: Penguin, 1976) (*TRM*).

La Maison de Claudine (Paris: Livre de Poche/Librairie Hachette, 1960) (*LMC*); *My Mother's House* and *Sido*, trans. Una Vincenzo Troubridge and Enid McLeod (Harmondsworth: Penguin, 1966) (*MMHS*).

La Naissance du jour (Paris: Flammarion, 1984) (*LNJ*); *Break of Day*, trans. Enid McLeod (London: The Women's Press, 1979) (*BD*).

'Le Patriarche' in *Bella Vista* (Paris: J. Ferenczi et fils, 1937); 'The Patriarch' in *The Rainy Moon and Other Stories*, ed. Antonia White (Harmondsworth, Penguin, 1976) (*TRM*).

Sido, suivi de Les Vrilles de la Vigne (Paris: Livre de Poche, Fayard/Hachette, 2004) (*SVV*).

Other Works Cited, Referred to, or Consulted

(Some French titles I read only in English translation, so in those cases I have given just those details.)

Crosland, Margaret, *Madame Colette: A Provincial in Paris* (London: Peter Owen, 1954).

Davis, Philip, *William James* (Oxford: Oxford University Press, 2022).

Francis, Claude, and Fernande Gontier, *Colette* (Paris: Librairie Académique Perrin, 1997) (*FG*).

Goudeket, Maurice, *Close to Colette*, trans. Enid McLeod (London: Secker & Warburg, 1957).

Jouve, Nicole Ward, *Colette* (Brighton: Harvester Press, 1987) (NWJ).

Kristeva, Julia, *Colette* (New York: Columbia University Press, 2004).

Marks, Elaine, and Isabelle de Courtivron (eds), *New French Feminisms* (New York: Harvester Press, 1986).

Milner, Marion, *A Life of One's Own* (London: Routledge, 2011).

Radway, Janice, *Reading the Romance: Women, Patriarchy and Popular Literature* (London: Verso, 1987).

Roberts, Michèle, *Cut Out* (Inverness: Sandstone, 2021).

Roberts, Michèle, *A Piece of the Night* (London: The Women's Press, 1978).

Roberts, Michèle, *Fair Exchange* (London: Little, Brown, 1999).

Roberts, Michèle, *Impossible Saints* (London: Little, Brown, 1997).

Roberts, Michèle, *Mud: Stories of Sex and Love* (London: Virago Press, 2021).

Roberts, Michèle, *Playing Sardines* (London: Virago Press, 2001).

Roberts, Michèle, *The Looking Glass* (London: Little, Brown, 2000).

Roberts, Michèle, *Une Glossaire/A Glossary, in During Mother's Absence* (London: Virago Press, 1993).

Sarde, Michèle, *Colette: Free and Fettered* (New York: William Morrow & Co., 1980) (CFF).

Thurman, Judith, *Secrets of the Flesh: A Life of Colette* (London: Bloomsbury Publishing, 2000) (SF).

Warner, Marina, *From the Beast to the Blonde: On Fairy Tales and their Tellers* (London: Chatto & Windus, 1994) (FBB)

INDEX